THE HIGH PRIESTESS'S VIGIL

ARCANA
Charity's Story

THE FOOL'S PATH

THE MAGUS'S HOUSE

THE HIGH PRIESTESS'S VIGIL

More Coming Soon!

THE HIGH PRIESTESS'S VIGIL

H. T. Brady

ARCANA: THE HIGH PRIESTESS'S VIGIL
Copyright © 2018 H. T. Brady
All rights reserved.

Published by H. T. Brady
www.arcananovels.com
ISBN: 978-1-7324001-2-2
First Edition: August 2018

Cover Illustration and Design by
Kaija Saaremäel and Silver Saaremäel

For Kaija and Silver.
Yes, you get this one too.

Prologue

Delia and I talked sometimes about where we'd go, if money and time were no object. I liked the idea of Bali. Beaches and oceans for me. For Delia it was always Paris. She imagined us strolling down cobbled streets, getting caught in the rain, and sipping espresso in fashionable cafes—even though she doesn't like espresso. She was good at making it sound nice—even the 'caught in the rain' part—and at getting me to catch her ambitions.

Now, here I was in Paris without Delia. I was pretty sure it was Paris, anyway.

She'd kill me. If she didn't already think I was dead.

She probably thought I was dead.

Which—on balance—was better than my actually being dead. But still not great.

My short-lived attempt to unite the Court of Wands against my mother—the Queen of Wands—had ended spectacularly poorly. I'd only managed to escape with my life because I had an extra tarot card from a... friend? I wasn't sure how to think of Hector. The Court of Wands and the Court of Swords were at war with each other, and being a Wand myself I wasn't entirely sure that I could count Hector—who would soon be the Two of Swords—as a friend. On balance though, he hadn't tried to kill me when he got a chance—so he was better than my family, right?

Looking back, with everything I know now, it's hard to remember how despairing I was just then—to portray how awful it was and how hopeless everything seemed—standing alone in a foreign city, in a foreign world.

In that moment, I wasn't thinking about how it could get worse.

Which was a mistake.

ONE

Rain in the Streets of Paris

I CLOSED MY EYES AND TRIED to enjoy the sound of the rain.

I was standing on some street in Paris—under the awning of a cafe filled with coffee and pastry I couldn't afford—while the rain struck the fabric over my head and pattered down idyllically on cobbled stones around my feet.

I'd come out of the catacombs only an hour or so ago, the same catacombs I'd magically dragged myself to in order to escape my mother. After she'd admitted to murdering my father and tried to kill me.

Of the many things I did not have, a way back to the City was the most pressing. I might have been able to work a traveling spell if I'd had my tarot deck. My deck had been stolen from me along with my focus—a tool for amplifying my magic. I still had my new control over my fire magic, but it wasn't exactly useful in this situation.

I was ready to set something on fire, just for the fun of it. I might have too, but I was scared that using fire magic might let my mother find me using the Ace of Wands—the heart of the power of the Suit of Wands. I was linked to the Ace, which is what gave me power over fire.

So. No tarot deck. No fire magic. No money. Nowhere to sleep. Right.

I did have a piece of Hector's card left—the two of swords—it was only a burnt corner, but I was still holding onto it.

The rain spent itself and I started walking. Walking made it easier not to cry—and I didn't want to fucking cry. I didn't know where I was going. Moving felt good and it warmed me up. At least my clothes were semi-appropriate. I didn't look exactly normal—but my black clothing and grey coat didn't stand out the way some of my Wands' clothing would have.

I wondered how the Queen and Ten of Wands would say I'd died.

It might be easiest to say that I died in the Magus's house. However, I thought my mother would prefer to blame Swords. Delia might believe that too. She'd been angry at me when I went back to the Magus's house the last time—she was sure it was a trap. I didn't want to think about that fight—if my mother managed to kill me, that would be our last conversation.

I wouldn't die, World damn it.

I needed a plan.

I could try to get to the airport, and see if I could get back to the airport in the City. That was how I'd arrived the first time. Of course, my mother was probably watching the airport in the City. Besides, I didn't have the appropriate card, but maybe... I looked down at the fragment of Hector's card. It was the slimmest of slim chances that it could help me, but that was all I had.

I kept walking.

Other options: a place like Paris probably had a dozen connection points with the City. The people of the City liked landmarks, and the distance between the City and the mundane world was less in those places that existed in both worlds. Conceivably, I could get back through the catacombs, Notre Dame or perhaps somewhere like the Eiffel Tower or the Louvre. Of those, I thought that Notre Dame might be my best bet—it was the most likely not to charge an entry fee.

Of course, I had no idea where Notre Dame was.

I kept my eyes out for a shop that looked like it might have a map.

It wasn't a good plan—I wasn't sure I could get myself back to the City without whole cards or my focus or some other help, but it was worth a try. Maybe the Fool would hear me—I was still theirs, after all.

I passed a bookshop. I was getting pretty cold, even with my thick clothes—the wind whistled down the narrow alleys and filled in the streets like water filling cracks in the sidewalk. I noted the street name, and walked into the bookshop in search of a map. I wouldn't be able to buy it, but I could figure out where I was.

I circled between the shelves without any luck, and then went down a short set of stairs— into a lower level. There were more shelves to search, but a table display caught my eye.

Tarot cards.

They weren't made in the City—they'd be weak, but it was better than nothing. I'd have a better chance of getting through...

I was standing and staring at them, wondering if I could grab a deck and run, when my mother revoked my connection to the Ace of Wands. She tore away my fire magic.

TWO

Quenched

I'D BEEN CONNECTED TO THE magic of the Ace of Wands since I was a child. I don't remember when my mother baptized me into the magic of fire—I couldn't remember a time before I had fire magic. I hadn't realized— I didn't know—

I woke on the floor of the bookshop, feeling like my guts had been scooped out. It hurt so much that it took my breath away—couldn't even scream or cry. I focused on not dying.

I was no longer a part of the House of Wands.

Someone was speaking to me, and I couldn't understand them. It took me a long, long horrible moment to realize that it wasn't because of the pain, but because they were speaking French.

I tried to smile and grimaced instead. I struggled up against gentle hands and pushed myself to my feet, speaking in as soothing a voice as I could as I pulled myself up the stairs and staggered out into the street.

"I'm fine," I said, over and over—willing it to be so, desperate to make it true. They left me alone. I made myself stand up straight in the street. The clouds were coming back.

"I'm fine," I told them, but the clouds didn't answer. I was shaking with the pain and it took all my strength not to curl up in a ball right there. I wasn't fine. On top of that I felt cold, a bone deep chill like the heat from my body had been leeched away—like I was bleeding out.

I hadn't realized how integral my connection to the Ace of Wands was. It had been like having an organ I could safely ignore—I hadn't realized I had it until she'd torn it out.

I had no illusions about who had done this. The King wouldn't do it—and the Queen would be lying to the Knight about my death. I had to believe that. He'd promised to protect Delia.

My mother had exiled me from the House of Wands.

"I'm fine," I whimpered. I started walking because it was that or lie down and die. Absurdly, I tried to 'walk off' having my heart cut out. What else was there to do?

I tried to keep my head up, but I was dizzy. I felt better if I stared at my own feet, focusing on taking the next step, over and over and over again.

If I was walking, then I wasn't dead.

It worked all the way to the river.

Then I made a mistake—I walked to the middle of

one of the bridges and stopped, turning to lean on one of the railings. I shouldn't have stopped moving. All the momentum went out of me. I doubled up against the railing, breath coming in little ragged sobs while my vision swam and got dark at the edges.

Rage rose in me—but there was no magic connected with it. No fire.

Fuck her. I'm not dying here. I'm not dying. We're not done. I'm fine.

I gritted my teeth— but being pissed off didn't keep me from shaking. It didn't stop the pain. I shoved myself up and off the railing, turning to keep walking. I got a few steps before falling over.

I don't remember falling—I just remember opening my eyes and seeing very distinctly the sandy texture of the concrete right beside my eye.

People clustered around me. There were low murmurs in French and someone tried to roll me over. There seemed to be some discussion of whether that was a good idea or not.

I didn't have it in me to care.

It had started raining again, and I had the impression of umbrellas swarming over me—blocking out the sky.

Abruptly, the pain lessened. I blinked.

"She's fine," said someone standing over me. "She's my friend. I've got her." I didn't know the voice.

Don't get me wrong, I still felt like hell— but my vision came back and the throbbing pain in my gut subsided enough that I thought I might be able to sit up again. In a minute.

"Charity Waits?" said the voice, urgent. "Can you get up?"

I had to work to pull the speaker's face into focus, and when I did I thought that—better as I felt—I might still be sick.

It was the Princess of Swords.

Unexpected Rendezvous

"CHARITY?" SAID THE PRINCESS of Swords again, sounding anxious. "I need you to get up. Can you move?"

"I think so," I said, still shaking. Part of me was sure I was about to get stabbed, and part of me was relieved that it wasn't my mother.

The Princess helped me up. She said something comforting to the few dubious onlookers—a few with their phones out. I caught the quick flash of a card in her free hand and I watched their eyes glaze over as they dispersed. She wore a sky blue overcoat that flared from her hips. Her black hair was held away from her dark face by a silver embroidered band and then flared around her face. This was the third time I'd seen her. The first time she'd sort of tried to kill me. The second time had been in a memory, when another Princess—the Princess of Wands—had died.

She held one of my arms and had me around the waist—crouching because she was taller than me.

"Come on, let's get away from here," she said, glancing around at the handful of tourists and Parisians.

"So you can kill me?" I asked. I tried to say it flippantly, but the words came out bitter.

Misty rain beaded in her hair, and she didn't look at me. The buttons on her coat were ornate silver, showing two mirrored women, twins, clasping each other's forearms.

"No," she said, and pulled me along another few steps. It took me this long to realize that she had a card in one hand. She was healing me—or at least keeping me upright. I didn't feel healed exactly— more like I'd gotten a jolt of a particularly potent energy drink.

"What are you doing here then?" I asked, each question its own stubborn kind of victory.

"I came to find you," she said. "Hector felt it— when you used his card."

Hector. He'd given me that two of swords so that I could get in touch with him. I'd lost the last fragment of it somewhere between here and the bookshop I'd collapsed in.

"Why?" I asked. "If not to kill me..."

She turned to me briefly as we kept walking—our faces uncomfortably close—and lifted one eloquent eyebrow as though to say 'we covered this already, I'm not here to kill you'. We continued in silence for awhile, making it to another intersection.

"Because," she said, choosing to answer my question as we paused before crossing a street. "I think you know who is fueling the feud between the Swords and the Wands."

Wind whistled down the streets and across the river beside us. I was still abominably cold.

"My mother," I said.

"Your mother," said the Princess.

"She promised to kill you," I said.

The Princess nodded, she picked our direction and kept us limping along.

"Why?" I asked.

"You don't know?" she asked, genuinely surprised.

"Nope," I said, panting.

"It's a long story," said the Princess.

"Aren't they all?" I asked.

"I'll tell you when we're back in the City," she said, her lips quirked up and she glanced at me sidelong again.

"So what do you want?" I asked. I tried to straighten up, but flinched when I did. The Princess of Swords 'tsked' under her breath and muttered about the oppressiveness of the mundane world.

"I want you to come with me to the Palace of Swords. I want you to help us stop this before anyone else gets hurt. I'd like to keep you alive and on the Fool's Path."

"I'm not on the Fool's Path anymore," I said. I couldn't be, could I? I wasn't a part of the House of Wands.

"There's only one way off the Fool's Path, aside from finishing the walk," said the Princess. "You're not there. Not yet."

"And if I don't want to go to the Palace of Swords?" I said. It was a childish thing to say, but my stubborn streak didn't like how little choice I was having here.

The Princess of Swords stopped and we swayed on the sidewalk together.

"You're serious?" she asked, in irritated disbelief. "I can leave you here to die, if you prefer. You might survive long enough for the Queen of Wands to come find you and make sure you're dead— she can finish you off however she likes."

"I'm sorry," I said. Thinking through the pain—even the lessened pain—was hard. "I'm sorry. You're helping me, and I— thank you."

"You're welcome," she said, grim. Then the corner of her mouth went up again. "I can't wait for you to meet *my* Queen. I'm going to need to be there for that. Come on—we've got a ways still to go."

"Where are we going?" I asked.

"We need to cross close to my Palace," she said, but didn't elaborate further.

So I limped along with the Princess of Swords, leaning on her and trying not to trip her or slip on the slick streets and sidewalks.

It wasn't ideal, by any means, but at least I had my way back to the City. All I had to do was figure out how to stay alive from one minute to the next. Then I would absolutely make the Queen of Wands regret fucking with me. I'd get back to Delia. I could do this. I had to.

FOUR

Bad to Worse

THE PRINCESS OF SWORDS AND I made an odd couple, shuffling along the streets of Paris— her in her neat sky blue coat and thick heeled boots and me in my grey jacket, dirt and dust from the catacombs clinging to my damp garments. Eventually, she was able to let go of my waist, and I could keep pace with her while holding onto her arm.

The Princess lead us to the subway. I did a double take when she produced ordinary euro from her pocket. She managed to buy us two tickets from the machines without letting go of me and then took us to stand on the underground platform. We stood well back from the tracks. A few commuters gave the Princess a second glance, but other than that the situation felt weirdly mundane. I tried, briefly, to come up with something to say—another question to ask—and couldn't. I gave it up and focused on standing.

We boarded a car, crushing in with the locals and the tourists. We were pressed together—packed in tightly. It was the opposite experience to another train ride, not so long ago, with the Knight of Wands. I thought briefly that we would be going to the airport.

While we were on the train, I took a quick inventory of how I felt. I was steadier on my feet and getting used to the pain. Without walking to distract me, I prodded mentally at the space where my magic had been. It felt better. Not healed, but better.

I let go of the Princess of Sword's arm—

—and gasped as the pain rushed back in. The tear in my magic was raw and viciously painful. My teeth clacked uncomfortably together—I was freezing cold.

"Don't do that!" hissed the Princess of Swords, grabbing my arm and supporting me. I tried not to be sick.

She'd been pouring magic into me, all this time—a steady stream of power funneled through the card in her hand. She held it against my arm—holding both me and the card. We swayed on the train and stared at each other.

I went back over what the Princess of Swords had said: *There's only one way off the Fool's Path, aside from finishing the walk. You're not there. Not yet.*

The words caught up to me properly now.

"I'm dying," I said, looking up at the Princess. "You're not healing me, you're keeping me upright."

She met my eyes steadily. *I'm right.*

"Being cut off from the Ace—exiled—it'll kill me?" I spoke remarkably calmly, if I do say so myself.

"Not always," said the Princess of Swords, serious.

"Don't give up. We'll get you to the Palace and get help. You're going to make it."

"Damn right, I am," I snarled, thinking of my mother. I tightened my grip on her arm. She didn't seem to mind.

We got off the train at a stop called 'Champs de Mars-Tour Eiffel'. When we came out of the subway, my eyes were immediately drawn up to the Eiffel Tower. The Princess of Swords started walking along the sidewalk by a busy street, towards the tower with me in tow. All the pictures of the Eiffel Tower I'd seen were taken from a distance. Up close, it was more air than iron—girders of a dozen different widths formed the impression of a lacy fractal. The structure was surprisingly delicate.

I wondered where the Eiffel Tower was in my City. I hadn't seen it—which wasn't really a surprise. I wondered if there was a map of the City. I'd used cards to navigate or been shown the way by denizens familiar with the place we were going. Absurd, really.

I missed my tarot deck.

The Princess bought us tickets to walk to the second floor of the tower. The cold and rainy weather meant that most sane folks were taking the elevator, so there wasn't much of a wait.

"Walking?" I asked. "Really?" I was exhausted, even with all the power I was borrowing from the Princess.

She looked grim. "I know. The stairs are the easiest way to cross back though. I can help you more once we're back in the City. I always forget how grating using magic is here."

My legs shook as I glanced up. We started up the stairs, slow and steady, our footfalls echoing on the metal steps.

I leaned on the railings with one arm and kept hold of the Princess of Swords's wrist with the other. She in turn held my wrist, with the card I still hadn't seen pressed against me.

I thought about my mother. She'd tried to kill me twice. It wasn't going to fucking work out for her.

One turn up the stairs and the wind joined us—screaming through the wire cage. I was so cold. We kept climbing. As we cleared the roofline, I glanced sideways. Paris—the buildings, the river and the park below—stretched around us in chilly beauty. Everything seemed suddenly to be so utterly ridiculous that I couldn't help but start laughing.

The Princess turned back to me, concerned. We paused on the stairs.

"What is it?" she asked.

I shook my head, and took another step—laughing while I hauled myself up those stupid freezing stairs. I stumbled onwards and she kept glancing back—the littlest frown creasing her brow.

"I'm in Paris," I finally managed to say, "Climbing the Eiffel Tower with you!"

I thought that was pretty funny.

"I see..." she lied. She didn't get it.

"This is Paris! The City of Love? It's supposed to be romantic. Or at least idyllic. Somewhere you go with someone you care about. I'm here with someone who tried to kill me. I mean, not the only person who has tried to kill me, but still... It's a small club. For now anyway. If I don't die, maybe it'll be a bigger club." That seemed funny too, and I kept giggling.

At first I thought that the Princess was concerned because she thought I'd lost my mind, but instead she stepped down so she was right in front of me. I stopped laughing, suddenly nervous.

"Charity," she said, very seriously, "I never wanted to kill you."

"Oh," I said. She still held my hand. "That's ah... good to know." She was saving my life now, so I might have forgiven her if she'd confessed to trying to murder me. This was nicer. Still.

I said, "Your Knight did though. Like, yesterday."

She was surprised. "He wasn't supposed to—," she said. "He was trying to kidnap you, which may not be much consolation. He did try to kill you at your presentation party, certainly. "

"And before I got to the City?" I asked.

"Yes."

"Does he know you're here?" I asked.

The Princess wobbled her head from side to side, as though to say 'yes-and-no': "He might know by now, I suppose."

"But probably not?"

"Probably not," The corner of her mouth tugged up again.

I huffed out a sigh. "Great," I said.

She glanced around us. We had the stairs to ourselves.

"I'm going to take us back now," she said. "It'll split my concentration—so the healing might weaken for a moment. Just hang onto me. Ready?"

"Sure," I said, nervous— afraid of the pain. She reached into her pocket and pulled out an eight of wands—the same card the Knight of Wands had used all that time ago to get me from the mundane world to the City.

She held the card differently than we did in Wands—squeezed between her index and middle finger on the right side of the card with her thumb stuck out like a reversed letter 'L'.

She focused on the card in her hand and tugged on my arm. We started walking up again. I had to close my eyes and walk blindly to keep the vertigo at bay. We were climbing into the City.

FIVE

No Place Like Home

THE VIEW SHIFTED AS WE CLIMBED, changing from the cold grey beauty of Paris in winter to the hodgepodge jungle of monuments and buildings of the City. We'd left Paris in the early afternoon, and incongruously arrived in the City in twilight. Neon zigzagged across the buildings around and below us. The City was alive and humming. I couldn't tell if it was as cold or colder than the mundane world—the loss of my magic made it hard to tell.

Despite everything, it was a relief to see all that beautiful chaos.

We reached the second floor of this false Eiffel Tower at the same time that we arrived fully in the City. I found myself on a promenade. There was a man waiting for us, standing in profile with the curve of his close shaved head showing sharp and clean against the sky. He turned from his view of the skyline towards us, and I recognized Hector.

21

"Charity!" he exclaimed, rushing forward. He stopped short, horror spreading over his face.

"What's wrong with her?" he asked the Princess.

"The Queen of Wands exiled her," she said, curtly. "Can you take over with the four of swords? I need a minute."

"Oh World," he whispered and drew a card from his deck—the four of swords—and offered me his arm. The Princess passed me over to him. Hector took over the spell smoothly—it didn't hurt. The Princess let out a relieved sigh as she straightened, stretching her arms above her head.

Hector seemed concerned, but also like he didn't know which question to ask first. I was smiling at him without really meaning to.

"What is it?" he finally asked.

"You did know, the whole time, didn't you? That I wasn't Delia." He'd never called me 'Charity' before now. I'd told him my name was Delia when we'd met.

He looked embarrassed. "Yes," he said. "Sorry about that."

Did you tell the Knight of Swords where he could find me? Did you almost get me kidnapped—or killed? I chuckled. I might have been better off, if I'd been kidnapped by the House of Swords.

I didn't ask then. There would be time later, hopefully, and right now I was relieved to see a familiar and friendly face. We'd survived the Magus's house together. That had to be worth something?

"Did you bring the cloaks?" asked the Princess.

"Yes, Highness" said Hector, indicating a bench near where he'd been standing. The Princess walked over to it, rolling her neck. Whatever she'd been doing had taxed her strength. She hadn't shown it until now. She kicked a bag out from under the bench and after a quick rummage she pulled out two large capes. They were dark blue with creamy silk linings and swords picked out at the hems in gleaming white.

The Princess of Swords threw hers over her shoulders and pulled up the hood, hiding her face, then she helped me on with mine. I'd never worn a cape before. I wrapped the rich fabric around myself, feeling worn out but warmer.

"Ready?" asked the Princess. "Can you handle the spell awhile longer?"

"Yes, Highness," Hector said, and then to me: "Come on, Charity. It's going to be okay."

There was a falseness to his optimism that scared the hell out of me.

Hector led me into the elevator and we rode down to street level in the City.

"Through the bazaar?" asked Hector.

The Princess said, "I've got us warded—but even without that, I don't think anyone will recognize her. She's not well known and they'll see the cloak."

Hector nodded and we plunged into the City. Peripherally, past the edge of my hood, I noticed that we went from a lantern hung street filled with swirling steam from a few food vendors, into a large open doorway. We walked along a stone arcade with little alcoves—each taken over by a merchant of some kind. The noise of shoppers and shopkeepers ricocheted through the plaster-painted arches, creating a dizzying clamor that came from all sides at once. Many of the people wore a sign of their allegiance to Swords.

I tried to pay attention to where we turned, but it was useless. It was all I could do to keep walking. The arcade became a blur, the scents of honey and then spices reaching me through my mental fog.

"A penny," a voice cut through the other voices of the market and I stopped, dragging Hector to a halt. The Princess of Swords bumped into us. "A whistle," the voice continued. "A whisper, a dream or a weed." It was sing-song, the voice seesawing up and down and running a serrated edge through my mind.

There was a woman seated between two of the alcoves, her back to a column. She was crunched into the space between an enormous basket and a pile of neatly folded jewel-toned scarves.

She wore veils, a hundred diaphanous layers hiding her from view.

"Charity?" asked Hector.

"A truth, a song, a pebble or heart's ease," the veiled woman sang to me. Spread at her feet on a black cloth were a hundred little silver crescents—pins and pendants and earrings.

She looked up at me and said, very clearly: "You can't see me."

"Give me the spell," commanded the Princess of Swords, taking my arm from Hector— smoothly switching over again. I hardly noticed.

"I can," I insisted to the veiled woman. She said nothing, her singing silenced.

"What?" asked the Princess, sounding worried.

"I can see her," I said, pointing.

A pause, and then: "There's no one there," said the Princess. "Charity, we need to move."

I glanced back at her in irritation.

"She's right there," I insisted. But I'd looked away. Oh, never look away from something important in the City until you are done with it.

When I turned back, the woman in her veils was gone.

I stood my ground for another moment, staring at the second basket that filled the space where she'd been.

"Hector," said the Princess, "Go tell them what's happened. The Four and the Queen and no one else. She's fading."

"I am not," I argued, but Hector ignored me and sprinted off into the crowd. "There was someone there!"

"I don't doubt it," said the Princess. "Take another step for me? Okay?"

"I can walk," I said, stubborn and annoyed that she was talking to me like a child. I started walking again and fell against her.

"What..."

The Princess of Swords set me on my feet, one arm around my waist again. She half carried, half walked me forward while I tried to understand why my feet weren't working properly.

I caught the flash of a card as she drew another to add to the spell holding me together. She used Strength—the image showed a woman with a lion—a Major Arcana. My mind cleared and I was able to take most of my own weight as we staggered out of the stone arcade. I also got another moment of clarity about my condition—it was taking serious magic just to keep me limping along.

It was full dark outside the bazaar. We started passing guards in the livery of the House of Swords. They stepped out of our way as though we were expected. Everyone let us pass.

We reached the entrance to a more modern building.

I tilted my head back, peering up. It was four sky-scrapers, towers with curved and scalloped edges. From the sky, they would have looked like flowers. They were joined by bridges criss-crossing between them at differ-ent floors.

Then we were inside, passing more guards and glass doors with slick white tiles under our feet. I got a vague impression of white stone and silver doors.

"Charity," said the Princess, "I'm going to put you to sleep. Do you understand? It's going to be easier to help you that way."

Part of me thought that was a truly excellent idea. I could sleep. I could rest for days and days and days. Part of me remembered being put to sleep by the Ten of Wands earlier today though—oh World, it was only ear-lier today—and rebelled.

The rebellious part won.

"No," I said, struggling against the magic she was pouring into me. "I don't want to. I—"

"Charity!" said the Princess of Swords. She kept say-ing my name. Why did she keep saying my name? "Listen to me!"

I blinked. I was facing her—when had she turned me?—staring into her brown, almost black, eyes.

"You survived the first shock of exile, but this is about to get bad. I want to help you, but you're making it harder. Even now you're strong enough to make this dangerous if you fight my help. Stop being a stubborn idiot and let me help you."

"She tried to kill me," I said, not sure why that mattered right now. It did somehow.

"I know," said the Princess. "She's not going to manage it though. Okay?"

"Okay," I said, and stopped fighting her.

SIX

Initiation

To be entirely honest, I don't remember much from my first few days in the Palace of Swords. I remember that everything hurt. I remember flashes of Hector and the Princess of Swords—both worried and tired. I remember a woman whose face I never saw—she had extraordinarily long hair and that was the sum of my impression of her. I dreamt that other people were there too—my mother, Delia, the Knight and King of Wands. I have a bad feeling I spoke to those illusions, or maybe screamed at them.

Magic fluctuated around me while I lay in bed—it rose and fell and tried to fill in the gap where *my* magic should have been. I knew, in a distant way, that it wasn't working. I was dying slowly, and the House of Swords was trying to save me. And failing.

The first thing I remember clearly again was cold wind on my face.

"Another minute," said the Princess of Swords in my ear. I got the impression that she'd been talking to me for longer than that—but I hadn't been able to hear it. I was standing up—I thought I was in an elevator. The floor was rising anyway.

The wind buffeted us. I tried to keep my feet steady, but the slick marble under them didn't give me a whole lot of purchase and I wasn't in the best shape. I entertained, briefly, the thought that I was about to be tossed off a building.

"Are you going to throw me off the tower?" I asked, vaguely curious.

"No," said the Princess of Swords, firmly. I got the added impression that I'd been asking that sort of question of her a lot.

I looked up.

We were outside, standing high on the top of one of the four towers that served as the palace for the House of Swords. Around us was air, and I couldn't see a way down. The floor itself must have risen.

Wind roared around us with alarming strength, but the Princess of Swords held me upright and redirected the air casually around us with her magic.

"I don't like this," said someone I didn't know. He was tall and lean, with a disapproving frown on his face.

"It's the last chance," said another stranger. She was small and old, with wispy white hair and warm brown skin. Her cane was shaped like a sword—carved from black wood to look like a scimitar.

I squinted and got a proper view of them. They were the King and Queen of Swords.

The King approached me. His worried expression intensified.

"Charity Waits," he said. "Will you join the House of Swords?"

I started laughing. In the crazy way.

"Even if she said 'yes' right now," said the Queen of Swords behind him. "It would not satisfy you. The choice is to let her go or try this—and it's ours to make, not hers."

His mouth twisted and he swirled away from me across the rooftop—is it a rooftop, if it's a hundred stories off the ground?

"And this is your decision?" he said, washing his hands of the responsibility.

"Yes," said the Queen of Swords, confident.

"So be it," he said, emotion gone from his voice. He put out a hand and the floor beneath us began to glow.

I turned away, blinded briefly. Then I felt power— power right there in front of me. I turned eagerly back, willing the spots from my eyes, casting about for the power I felt. I needed it.

A sword stuck out of the blue marble floor. It was enormous, for a sword, taller than the King of Swords and it burned with energy in the sunlight. It made the empty place in me hurt worse—ache with wanting my power back, and willing to take any power to fill that void. I forgot about the air around us, about the fall, and about everyone else in the world. I wanted the Ace of Swords.

I would have stepped forward, but the Princess of Swords had me. I tried to shake her off. She gritted her teeth and held on. "Charity," she said, half warning and half plea.

The Queen stood by, watching, and the King of Swords raised one hand—holding his ace of swords card—and extended the other up to the hilt of the Ace of Swords itself.

My breath sped up. The Princess of Swords was still pouring power into me to keep me from feeling the pain of my exile. I tried to be patient, tried to look at anything but the Ace. It didn't work.

The King of Swords summoned the aura of his own card. He grew in my eyes, and was wreathed in clouds and dressed in indigo and iridescent blue. He was regal, his eyes keen and clear and brilliant—and he reached out to the Ace of Swords. All the power of the Ace—all the power that I wanted—started to pour into him. I whined, jealous and desperate to be made whole with that magic. It was all right there, so close.

The Princess used her own weight to keep me in place.

The King extended his hand with the card in it towards me.

The magic of the Ace of Swords felt cold, at the edge of my mind, and hard.

"She's going to break free," said the Princess of Swords, tense and afraid. The wind was screaming around us.

In myself, I felt the raw, raw edge of where the fire used to be.

Turns out, air wasn't at all like the fire.

Power lanced from the card in the King's hand into my chest.

For a moment, we were connected, he and I. I saw *him*—saw a spider thin scar that poked up out of his collar, saw that his eyes had hazel in them, that his shoulder hurt and had hurt for a long, long time, and saw that he liked reading and writing. I saw the mild disappointment he felt all the time for the inevitable flaws of human nature around him and the struggle he felt to love them anyway, even and especially his Court.

Then the power pouring from him started to pool in me—started to fill in fast. Too fast. There was too much of it, and it felt wrong—like someone was trying to fit a round peg into a too small square hole somewhere right around my gut. The magic stretched and tore out a space for itself without mercy. I shrieked, and my knees folded. The Princess let go of me and was yelling something.

I wasn't looking at the Ace anymore. I crushed my eyes closed and screamed and thrashed against the cold marble.

I don't know how long it took.

The next thing I remember, after the pain, was someone trying to uncurl me. I was on the floor still, but there were walls around me again.

They'd carved whatever shape I had been into something else. The sharp, bleeding pain was dimmed.

The Court of Swords spoke above me. I heard the Princess ask the Queen: "Did you know it would be like that?"

"No," said the Queen, somewhere out of my sight. "I've never claimed someone from another House before. No one, to my knowledge, has. It was a calculated experiment. But an experiment nonetheless."

"Did it work?"

"We'll find out."

SEVEN

Recovery

I WOKE UP IN THE MIDDLE of the night. I didn't know where I was and tried to get up quickly.

Everything hurt still. I whimpered and fell back to the bed, holding as still as I could and hoping and hoping that that would make it stop hurting.

"Shh..." said a woman's voice. She smoothed my hair back. She smelled like incense and old books. She'd been singing moments before—there were echoes of her voice lurking in the room somehow.

"What happened?" I whispered, blinking in the dark. I couldn't see her face.

"Pain and healing," she said. "Promises and breaking."

"Who are you?"

She didn't answer—I heard more than saw the swish of her long curtain of hair and of the veils. She sighed.

"You can't see me," she said, sadly.

"What?" I could, I thought. I *could* see her. Well, her shadow in the room.

"Go to sleep," she said.

I obeyed, falling back to sleep or to something close enough to it.

The next time I woke up, it was daytime. I was aware enough that I didn't try to leap up, but drew in a cautious experimental breath.

I still hurt and I felt... different. I'd become a Sword.

"Charity?"

I turned my head gingerly to look at Hector. His clothing was rumpled—baggy pants with a wide waist and a loose shirt in ivory and royal blue—like porcelain. He'd sat up to get a better look at me, leaning forward with an elbow on a knee and his chin resting in one hand.

"You're awake," he said, smiling his nice smile. "How do you feel?"

"Like I got hit by a semi," I said, honestly.

"A what?" he asked.

"A... chariot," I said, referring to one of the Major Arcana.

"Oh..." he said, not sure how to take that.

"It's an improvement," I said, trying to soften his worries. I wasn't actually sure that I was going to be okay, but it seemed like I had a good chance at it now.

He bobbed his head. "Good, good."

I turned my eyes around the room, wary of moving and filled with an exhausted apathy. Three walls were pale blue and one was almost entirely a window. Hector sat in a stiff white armchair beside my canopied bed— hung with silvery transparent fabric.

"Is that what it's like usually?" I asked. He didn't understand what I meant. "When someone joins the House of Swords?" I clarified.

"You don't remember? From when you joined Wands?"

"I was very young," I said.

"Oh."

"That's odd?" I asked. I didn't know.

"Well, granting young children power over elemental magic is... risky."

I supposed children with the power to play with fire whenever they wanted to might indeed qualify as 'risky'. I'd never thought about it. I laughed and then stopped when it hurt.

"It was rough," said Hector. "Joining the House is usually exhausting for the King and the initiate—tires you out for a few days—but the King only got out of bed yesterday."

My stomach sank. "How long?" I asked, dread creeping in. How long since they'd given me the power of the Ace of Swords? How long since my mother had tried to kill me?

"Umm..." Hector hesitated.

"World dammit, Hector, how long have I been out?"

"Almost a week," he said, quickly, getting it out fast.

"Oh fuck," I said. Tears welled in my eyes. "Delia."

"Delia?" asked Hector. "Charity, are you...?"

"She's been thinking I... She thinks I'm dead, and it's been a week..." I hiccuped. Everything hurt and I was still so, so tired. "She's going to be so mad at me." Looking back, I was crying as much about the pain as anything else. I was miserable and feeling lost and unstuck at the edges. I knew that it was a reasonable way to feel, but also that it didn't help anything.

Hector sat at the edge of my unhappiness, waiting and patient and not saying anything.

I sniffed and let the tears run down the sides of my face.

Hector stood up and pulled out a handkerchief. He dabbed the sides of my face carefully and still didn't say anything. He wore studs in his ears—silver swords.

"Thanks," I said, with a shudder.

"Sure," he said and he backed off to sit down again.

"What are you doing here?" I asked.

"We've been taking watches," said Hector, fiddling with his hands.

He smiled, wanly, and said, "I'd like to... I'd like to apologize, actually, properly. For what happened in the Magus's house. But now I'm worried that my timing is bad."

"Oh, it's fine," I said. I didn't care—I felt mildly benevolent towards anyone who wasn't actually trying to kill me at this point. With the crying out of my system, the apathy had come back.

"It was inevitable," said Hector, "However, I... didn't handle it well."

"In what way?"

"I should have told someone earlier," he said.

"What? You should have tried to get me killed sooner?"

"Killed!" he said, astonished. "No! It wasn't like that. He wouldn't— that wasn't why he—" He caught sight of my smile and gave a huff of relief, scratching his neat beard. "Huh. At least you can laugh about it." Then, he said: "The Knight, you know—I know there's no reason for you to know this—but he's a good... person."

I rolled my eyes towards him.

"He's your friend?" I asked, guessing that that last word had been a substitution.

Hector nodded. "He recommended me as the Two. We've known each other for a long time."

"I see," I said, not sure at all that I did see.

"What I meant, about telling someone earlier— after I met you I wasn't sure what to do. I knew pretty quick that you weren't training for the Magus and figured you were a Wand. After a day or two I was pretty sure you were *the Wand*, so to speak. And I just didn't want to tell ...anyone. It was nice to have a friend in the Magus's house, and I wasn't supposed to come back to Swords until I'd finished my training, so I figured it wouldn't be..." he shook his head and blew out a sigh.

"Do you know what the Two of Swords means?" he asked, momentarily diverted.

I thought about it for a minute. In my deck, it had been a card showing a woman balancing on a railing, blindfolded and with a sword in each hand. I'd used one of Hector's cards to change worlds, to switch from the world of the City to the mundane world, but it was the nature of twos—duality—that had done that. The card, more specifically, meant a problem with two well thought out perspectives. It could be consideration—finding a path—or overanalyzed deadlock.

"You over think things," I guessed, feeling fuzzy and sleepy again.

He nodded. "I know it's part of what makes me a good

candidate as the Two of Swords, but it's irritating too. Becoming a card involves facing things about yourself... but you know."

"Anyway—" he continued, "The Knight called me back, summoned me to the Palace of Swords and asked me straight out and I told him, and he came to try to capture you there. The Court wanted a numbered card from Wands, but you were almost as good a choice."

"Was he angry?" I asked. "That you hadn't come earlier?"

"Yes," said Hector, sounding weary. "I knew there would be politicking that would go with joining the Suit. I didn't expect it to become so complicated so quickly."

He'd stood up and was pacing, nervous and unhappy. "I'm sorry," he finished. "You're tired."

"Yeah," I said. I really was tired again. In fact, I was already nodding off. My body was truly annoyed with me. "It's nice to know someone cares what I think."

He opened and closed his hands.

"I do," he said.

"It's fine, Hector," I said, letting my eyes close. "Thank you."

EIGHT

Old Enemies

I WOKE AGAIN IN THE half-shadow of a new dawn—the sun peeking over the horizon outside my enormous window—to the sound of the door slamming open and the Knight of Swords yelling at someone.

I panicked.

I shot up in bed, turning towards the noise with hands raised to attack before I could think. I caught one quick glimpse of the Knight of Swords—his pale blonde hair, narrow face, and snarling expression—and I snatched up all the magic I could find and hurled it at him. A blast of air ran madly through the room, unfocused and uncontrolled. Paintings fell off the walls and the hangings on the bed went flying, the door slammed behind him, and he had to put up his own hands to ward off the storm. I, in turn, threw myself backwards off the bed and into the window. I slammed into the thick glass, the impact vibrating through my body and the room, as I slid down to the ground, hands still up.

It was an enormous amount of power, in one burst.

I sat stunned. It wasn't like fire. Fire was like being wrapped in the most excellent blanket while knowing that nothing in the world can stop you. This was like flying, to use air magic through the Ace of Swords.

For a moment, the Knight of Swords and I stared at each other.

"What the hell?" I yelled.

"How did— who brought you here?" he yelled in turn. He drew his sword—his focus—but he didn't seem to know what he wanted to do with it. Which was good for me. I'd burned most of the power I had in one go.

"Listen," I said, biting down hard on my temper.

The door snapped back open, and the Knight spun, weapon raised, turning with fury on the newcomer with his weapon. It was Hector. My friend threw his hands up, freezing.

"You!" hissed the Knight. "You knew she was here!"

"I did, Erik, I'm—"

"Don't apologize again," snapped the Knight, cutting him off. "Why wasn't I informed? How is she a *Sword*?"

Hector hesitated, searching for the right words. Meanwhile, I was torn between paying attention to the unfolding drama between them, finding out that the Knight of Swords *had* a regular name and that it was Erik, and the feeling of being a part of the House of Swords.

Admittedly, everything since I'd been exiled from the House of Wands had been awful and muddied—I already didn't remember much from it—but this relief from being whole and full of magic again, and yet changed, filled me with awe.

"Answer me," said the Knight, as footsteps sounded in the hallway again—running towards us.

I could see Hector's expression, struggling still with what to say. "It was the right choice..." he started, but the Knight cut him off with an angry gesture.

"My bitch mother kicked me out of Wands," I called from the floor, helpfully. "She tried to kill me. You two have that in common now."

The Knight spun back to me, his face set in hard and furious lines. "You— that's—"

Luckily, the footsteps turned out to be the Princess of Swords.

"Charity?" she called from the doorway. I waved to her from where I sat, mostly hidden behind the bed. I was too tired to try to get up yet.

The Princess ignored Hector and the Knight and came around the bed to check on me. The Knight spluttered, "You knew! Was the whole House aware? You know who's daughter she is! It's dangerous for you to be near her!"

The Princess of Swords didn't reply. Once she was sure I wasn't hurt, she offered me a hand up.

I chuckled.

"We've got to stop meeting like this," I said and was rewarded by the little lift at the corner of her mouth which was the way she smiled.

She got me back on my feet, for what seemed like the hundredth time.

The Knight of Swords stood at the center of the room, fuming. It seemed like a dozen feelings were warring in his face—from his hatred of me and my mother, to his instinct to protect the Princess of Swords, to his fury at being left out and his continued confusion about how the hell I'd ended up as a Sword.

"Charity isn't going to hurt me," said the Princess of Swords. "She and her mother are not on the same side."

"She was a Wand," said the Knight.

"*Was*," said the Princess. "The Queen exiled her."

That shut him up again for another moment. The way the Princess said 'exiled' and the way the Knight flinched made me think that there was more weight attached to that word than the pure cruelty of my mother's action.

"It could be a trick," he said, finally.

"It's not," said the Princess.

"You don't—"

"We're fairly confident of that," said a new voice. The Queen of Swords had joined the party in my room. Behind her stood two servants in the livery of the House of Swords—one was flushed, like she'd been running, and one carrying an enormous Sword. The weapon wasn't quite as big as the Ace had been, but it was close. The Queen glanced around at all of us. She seemed amused.

"So you knew as well," said the Knight, bitterly.

"I was going to tell you today," said the Queen to him. "Just not at quite such a stupid hour of the morning."

"You should have told me before she was allowed to join the House," he said.

"It wouldn't have changed my decision," said the Queen.

With an angry gesture the Knight of Swords sheathed his weapon. He glared around at all of us, his eyes settling on Hector.

"You'll need someone else to sponsor you to join the Suit, I think," he spat. Then the Knight strode angrily past his Queen and out of the room. His exit left a vacuum in the room—fear, magic and anger all rushing out with him.

Hector stood stiffly, eyes unfocused, hurt. The Princess said, more to the room than directly at Hector: "He'll come around. He doesn't like surprises."

Hector nodded absently.

The Queen let out a huff. "Well, apparently my day is starting earlier than I intended. Out, my dear Princess. And you, Hector. I suppose I may as well get acquainted with our newest Sword."

NINE

The Queen of Swords

HECTOR AND THE PRINCESS LEFT together. I thought I heard her say something comforting about breakfast, and my stomach rumbled. I was starving. The servant who'd clearly run around and woken up Hector, the Princess, and the Queen came in and cursorily picked up some of the things I'd blown over when I'd thrown my little storm at the Knight. She grunted as she heaved the armchair upright. I wanted to help, but I probably would have fallen over again trying.

The other servant came into the room and leaned the enormous sword against the wall before looking to the Queen. I realized that the monstrous weapon must be her focus.

"Bring us breakfast too, will you?" she said. "Something sweet. And extra for Miss Waits, I think."

He bowed and departed. The other servant sighed—

and I was reminded with a pang of Rosette—before going out the door too, closing it behind her. Which left me alone with the Queen of Swords.

My new Queen. I'd seen her when I was initiated into the House, but now I had a chance to study her more closely. She wore a robe, in a heavy white brocade that wrapped somewhat like a kimono. She seemed ancient but healthy. A place for her deck was clearly sewn into the overlarge sleeves of her robe. She used a cane—polished black wood in the shape of a curving scimitar.

The Queen walked—with a slight limp to her step—over to the armchair and sank into it, her hands on the top of her cane.

I sat on the bed, with the pillows mere feet behind me. The exhaustion dug in too, warring with my hunger, and I tried to sit up straight to keep myself alert.

The Queen looked at me critically, "How do you feel?" she asked. Her voice had a little creak to it.

"Not bad, considering."

"Not a thing many people recover from," she said, clicking her tongue sympathetically.

"I wouldn't say I'm recovered," I replied.

"Nor would I," conceded the Queen. She sighed and just considered me again. Her veins stood out on her hands, but her wrists and arms were strong. I wondered if she could actually lift the sword that had been left behind with her.

I let the silence stretch and then asked: "So, what exactly do you want with me?" No point beating around the issue.

"I'm not entirely sure yet, my dear," said the Queen.

"Have you had a chance to consider the strangeness of your position?"

"Not particularly," I said, honestly. "I was mostly occupied with not dying."

The Queen snorted. "You mean in fighting the people trying to help you."

I shrugged. "I'm sorry."

"Are you? We did save your life, you know."

I opened my mouth for a flippant reply. Then I took another look at the shrewd Queen and said, "I'm grateful—most especially to her Highness and to Hector. I get the feeling though that even if you aren't sure what you want in return that it's because you're considering more than one possibility— not because you don't have any ideas."

She smiled at me. "I think I like you, Charity Waits. Let's be straightforward. That's good. To go back to your position. You've survived being exiled and joining a new House, and you are still on the Fool's Path."

"Your Princess said that. That I'm on the Path. How is that possible now though? I can't be part of the Court of Wands now, and there's no place for me in the Court of Swords. What do I become, if I walk the Fool's Path and have no where to go at the end?"

"There are a few precedents," said the Queen. "If you survive."

"Like what?" I asked the question fast, like I was pulling off a bandage, before I could think about it too much.

"It's admittedly a rare occurrence. Very rarely the Major Arcana themselves need heirs, and that is how someone tries to take that position—by being exiled. It's a risk most aren't willing to take—though it's less likely to be fatal *after* surviving the Fool's Path, with the countenance of all the Major Arcana. When I was very, very young, the face of the Fool changed."

"So, I could become a Major Arcana?" I asked. That wasn't really helping my panic.

"Potentially. The City is a strange place—you might survive and be able to serve one of the Houses or another." She smiled a wicked smile. "Maybe the Queen of Wands will get her wish and there will be a vacancy for you here in the House of Swords before you finish the Path. You've a long way to go, my dear. Anything could happen."

I didn't want to think about that either. It must have been plain on my face, because the Queen said: "Not our immediate concern, truly."

"What is?" I asked, cautiously.

There was a knock at the door. The servant—the sword bearer—returned with a large tray of what smelled like cinnamon and honey pastries. At a gesture from the Queen, he set them on the desk and left again. With disarming happiness, the Queen selected a pastry and took a large bite, scattering crumbs as she did so. She smiled at me.

"Eat something, Miss Waits."

I reached for a pastry as the door closed once more behind her servant.

"Now," said the Queen of Swords. "Let's talk about what we're going to do about your mother."

TEN

Breakfast and Treachery

I STOPPED WITH THE PASTRY halfway to my mouth.

"You want to kill her?" I asked the Queen, worried by how easily the words came to me.

The old woman licked her lips, catching a few pastry crumbs and then nodded, "I'm going to destroy the Queen of Wands, and I'd like your help with that."

I took a big bite of the pastry to give myself time to think. As I considered, she continued:

"New Queens and Kings are sometimes bellicose," said the Queen of Swords. "Especially when they first take power. I had a nasty little war with the King of Disks when he first came to power. This is different. This has dragged on and sucked two Houses into what is essentially a personal matter. She's carrying it on with no sign of letting it go—and no particular concern for what's at stake for the rest of us."

I mimicked the non-committal head bobble the Princess of Swords had used. Honestly, it sounded close enough—but the Knight of Swords didn't seem like he was ready to let things go either.

"Now, I could just let this be a war between the Swords and Wands," said the Queen, "but that would end badly for both sides. Which seems unnecessary, since I think I know what the problem is. Or rather who. Now, I've gotten the impression that you didn't find your mother charming, particularly? Even when you were a Wand?"

"Was it the trying to kill me that tipped you off?" I said.

"Indeed," she said with a chuckle and a nod, confirming her own points. "How would you say the King of Wands feels about the Queen of Wands?"

I was torn for a moment. I was a Sword now. The Swords had saved my life. I also remembered this Queen talking about it. I wasn't sure how far her concern for my well-being stretched. Besides which, I still felt a loyalty to the King of Wands. I believed that he'd done his best to protect me, and I was fairly certain my mother had some sort of curse on him, a permanent spell called a 'seal' that kept him under control. Thinking of that made me worry about him—and about Delia and the Knight of Wands. I hoped they were sensible enough not to be investigating that right now.

I wasn't sure how much I wanted to share yet, but there was something in the way the Queen of Swords asked the question that made me think she already knew that my former King and Queen didn't particularly get along. So, I walked a middle road.

"How did you know?" I asked, confirming the split in the Court of Wands.

The Queen of Swords smiled again, pleased, and said, "A letter I received—when the Queen of Wands was 'dead'—from the King. It was actually with the invitation to your presentation at the Fool's pavilion. It made an overture to peace that I wasn't expecting."

I nodded.

The Queen snorted and added, "We actually thought it was part of a trap—that he was working with his Queen. Then everyone seemed so surprised when she reappeared. Shocked. We've had to rethink things."

"How did you know? That she wasn't really dead."

She sobered and flicked pastry crumbs from her lap. "The Knight of Swords swore an oath to kill your mother—a serious one with a Major Arcana to witness—"

"I saw it," I said. In the Magus's house, I'd watched him swear by Justice to kill my mother in a vision.

The Queen tilted her head and then said, "Ah, your focus. Yes. That was an ugly day."

"Is that how everyone gets their focus? Through a memory of their predecessor?" I asked. "No one told me."

The Queen smiled. "We can't— the Magus controls certain knowledge. If you try to talk about it with anyone other than a Court Card you won't be able to."

"Nice," I said, grumpy.

"It's not the only secret of the Fool's Path. You're on to the High Priestess then?" asked the Queen. "The very mistress of secrets... good luck."

"Thanks."

"We've wandered from the point," said the Queen. "We

knew the Queen of Wands lived because my Knight's oath still sat on him. If she'd died, he would have been free."

My turn to nod and put a few pieces together.

"So. The King and the former Princess-in-Waiting of Wands are not particularly well disposed to the Queen of Wands. The Knight is hers, but that's a weak enough Court for a coup."

"Actually..." I said, a little twist of my mouth betrayed my disagreement.

The Queen caught the tone immediately. "It's an open secret that the Knight of Wands is in love with his Queen," she said. "What changed?"

"She lied to him," I said with a shrug. "I can't promise that he'd stand against her—not now that I'm gone. However, when I left the Palace of Wands, he was more on my side and the King's, than on hers."

Delight lit up the old woman's face. "Well," she said. "How interesting."

I stared down at my hands, unable to rejoice in the weakness of the Wands. "How will you keep the Knight of Swords from continuing to escalate things? I'm not sure he'll be satisfied, with only my mother..."

"He'll have to be," said the Queen of Swords, abruptly grim. She sighed. "He'll grumble and sulk and he'll let it go. Mostly. I don't think you'll ever be friends."

I laughed hollowly. "Why does he hate her especially? What was that fight really about—between him and the Princess of Wands?"

The Queen was surprised. "That was about the former Princess of Swords."

Fuck.

"The one my mother killed—the one she let my—" I stopped. *Oh World damn. Damn it all.*

I frowned, thinking fast. I'd thought that my mother had let my father die—delayed rescuing him from the Swords because she had a shot at taking out the Princess of Swords. I thought she'd arrived too late. But she hadn't. She'd killed him. Why had she killed my father?

"She was the Knight's half-sister. The last Princess of Swords," said the Queen, watching me closely, as though she were trying to decide if I was playing dumb or not. "That's why he won't let it go."

Double fuck.

Outside, a cloud passed over the wintry sun, casting us both in shadow for a moment.

"You didn't know," said the Queen, genuinely surprised.

"No," I said. Then I shook it off. I needed to think this through on my own, but there was something more important for me to talk about with the Queen. If she was going to try to take down the Queen of Wands, then I knew what I wanted in exchange for my help.

"I need to let someone know I'm alive," I said. "I'll help against the Queen of Wands, but there's someone I need to protect."

"Your mundane world friend?" guessed the Queen.

Triple fuck.

"Delia," I confirmed, no point being circumspect on this one. "How did you know about her?"

"She was with you when my Knight first encountered you in the City. She was at your party, as well. We asked around."

"I need to let her know I'm alive," I said.

"No," the Queen of Swords shook her head.

"Why not?" I asked, irritation rising. It wasn't a lot to ask.

"Because right now the Queen of Wands thinks you are dead, my dear. That's how I want to keep it. It's how you want to keep it too, if you think about it for a moment."

I opened my mouth to argue, and then I did think about it.

"Is there any way you can make her safer than by giving your mother no reason to suspect you are alive?" said the Queen.

I drew in a calming breath and closed my eyes.

"There's got to be a way to safely tell her," I said. There had to be.

"Is there a way she could hide the knowledge, if the Queen is paying attention to her?"

Delia was a better liar than I was, but I knew—now, more than ever—that the old entrenched fear I felt for my mother was not unjustified.

Oh World, Dee, I'm so sorry. I tried not to think of the way we'd parted. She'd been angry at me for not telling her about Hector. She was going to throttle me. Assuming both of us lived to see the other.

"So..." I said slowly, "What you're saying is that you've only got it out for the Queen, my mother. You're not trying to burn the House of Wands to the ground?"

"An interesting choice of words, but yes. That's correct."

"And you want my help?"

She nodded. "Your mother is wily and irritatingly clever—but she has no reason to think you survived your exile. There's nothing in the mundane world that could have helped you." The Queen of Sword's lips curved like a knife's edge. "I think we can make you quite the upsetting surprise for her. I'll do my best to avoid collateral damage within the House of Wands. The sooner we act, the better chance of that I have."

"Then let's act fast," I said.

"Good," said the Queen, standing up. She gave me another of her critical looks, assessing me.

"Another day of rest first, I think," she said.

"I'm capable now," I said. "If we need to act fast—"

"Fine line between fast and stupid, my dear," said the Queen of Swords. "Let's be wary of crossing it."

ELEVEN

My Gilded Cage

After the Queen of Swords left, I crawled back into bed. It was still early morning and I thought I'd just close my eyes for a minute, but when I woke back up the sun said it was close to noon.

I hoisted myself out of bed and checked out the view from my enormous window. The City, in all its messy glory, spread out around me like an especially haphazard patchwork quilt in the light of day. I was very high up—the Fool would like it here. I could see the roof of the bazaar I'd come through with the Princess and Hector, along with the replica Eiffel Tower. Cathedral spires and minarets pierced the sky in the distance between stupas, plaster buildings, blue Greek domes and neon nonsense signs.

I couldn't see the Palace of Wands.

There was some irony in the idea that I'd returned to

the City because I thought my mother was dead, and now here I was— a vengeful ghost in the City I'd thought to leave behind forever. In my head, I tried to explain the situation to Delia, my gut clenching as I failed to come up with a sufficient apology for the situation.

What had the Queen of Wands told Delia, the King and the Knight about my death? Would they believe it?

And why had my mother killed my father?

I hadn't had time to wrestle with the revelation. My mother had not let my father die, but killed him. I couldn't think of a reason for her to lie about it this time—and I forced myself to remember that my mother was as good at spinning an unforeseen situation to her advantage as she was at setting her own schemes into motion.

I knew very little about my parents and their relationship. I rarely saw them together—I shook my head. Why was this so hard to remember? It wouldn't come into focus.

I shuddered even though I wasn't cold and caught a whiff of a scent of old books, a dusty library.

I whirled around, remembering the woman with the long hair who had been watching over me the first time I woke up. There was no one else in the room with me. Was that a dream? I hadn't seen her since I'd awoken properly.

Feeling twitchy and creeped out, I tried to distract myself by looking around my new room. I'd seen the main room, but in the daylight I noticed that along with the canopy the bed had a headboard carved with an ornate pattern of feathers and knives. The floor was stone—bluish slate—and a heavy, light-blocking black curtain hung at one end of my window. Helpful, if I didn't want to wake at the break of day every morning.

Next I tried the door to the outside world. It was locked. I wasn't surprised, but I was annoyed. I contemplated blasting the door with air—or trying to anyway—and decided against it. For now.

Like my room at the Palace of Wands, the wardrobe came with an assortment of clothing. That made me think of Delia. I stared at the dresses and slacks and robes in shades of white and blue and tried, unsuccessfully, to keep from seeing her face light up. *Let's try!* she'd say, and pick something for me and something for herself.

I went to check out the bathroom, moving to avoid thinking.

The bathroom looked like it came out of a modern millionaire's imagination—like what they thought an old roman bath might be like. The marble tub was sunk down into the floor like a pool. The fixtures were silver and one corner was devoted to a shelf full of fluffy white towels.

I suppose, if I had to be a prisoner, I liked being an honored prisoner.

I showered and changed into the simplest available clothing: a soft white tunic and pale blue leggings. Delia would not have approved.

Next, I wanted another try at my magic. I settled myself crosslegged on the bed, then steadied my breathing and poked at the magic with my mind.

It was distinctly odd. Continuing my organ metaphor for a moment—this was like I'd been given an extra set of lungs that I was learning to use. I stretched out a hand and thought about breathing through my palm.

I felt stirring in the air when I did that. A smile crept onto my face. It was good to have power back—immediate power at my disposal, without the need for cards. This at least, was an improvement—and something I had some control over.

I tried again, focusing on the feeling of breathing through my hand. I drew in and held a deep, deep breath, and concentrated. I imagined letting it all out in one gust from my hand.

A gratifying surge of wind answered me, rattling the curtain and slamming the bathroom door closed.

There was a quick step outside my door and it opened.

"Miss Waits? Are you okay?" A young woman with straight black hair and a neatly pressed Swords uniform stood there, seeming wary— like she was afraid I would try to break out. Not an unreasonable fear, given my earlier thoughts. She was the same servant who'd run to Hector and the others this morning. I tried a smile. She was younger than Rosette, back in the Palace of Wands.

"I'm fine," I said. "Sorry. Just trying some things out."

"You're sure?" she asked.

"Yes," I said, and she started to retreat out of sight. I stopped her with a question: "Wait a moment, what's your name?"

"Camilla, Lady," she said, and then: "I mean, 'Fool'." It was technically the proper way to address me, but still unsettling.

"Right," I said. "Would it be possible to get something to eat? And do you have any idea when I might expect to hear from the Court again? And, um, can I get a book or something? I'll go nuts in here by myself."

Camilla looked relieved that I was behaving so reasonably. "Is there a book you want? I was going to go get your lunch in a minute. Also, the Princess wondered if she could call on you this morning? I mean, afternoon now. Should I tell her you're awake?"

I nodded. "That would be very kind," I said, leaning on my City accent without meaning to. "And a book about Swords would be helpful, but anything really. Thank you."

"Yes, Fool," she said, and withdrew, closing the door behind her. I tried more carefully to summon gusts and eddies of wind and direct them around the room, thinking of the Magus and his card, and that—grudgingly—maybe I had learned something about discipline and practice.

TWELVE

Princesses of Swords

It was almost evening when the Princess of Swords came to see me.

I'd devoured my late lunch alone—a pile of fruit and several thin pieces of bread with a spicy chickpea mixture lavishly spread over them—and practiced air magic until I was exhausted. I sat down to read what Camilla had brought me—she'd chosen a hefty history of the House of Swords and a current serial romance that was apparently popular right now. I read the first of the serial that afternoon, before the Princess of Swords came to see me.

She had a packet of folded papers with her and wore a formal, almost militaristic white coat with tails. She'd tied her hair further back than usual, making it a sunburst of tiny brown curls.

"Feeling better?" she asked, sitting down in the chair

by the desk and setting down her papers. She studied me critically. It reminded me of the way the Queen had assessed me, and I wondered if it was a Swords' thing.

"Much much better," I said. "Thank you. The King of Swords?"

"Recovered," she said. "You surprised us all. No one thought it would be that brutal. Though I suppose we should have expected it—given the state you were in already."

"I know," I said. "I heard you talking. At least, I think I did. It hurt a lot."

Thinking about hearing them talking, I was reminded of the strange woman I'd seen in my room. I asked, "Who was taking care of me? When I was out?"

"I know Hector spent a bit of time with you," said the Princess. I nodded. "Mostly, you needed rest. Camilla, who's outside the door, stayed with you too. We all looked in, at one point or another."

"Camilla doesn't have the right hair," I said.

"What?"

"There was someone else—a woman with longer hair."

"You're sure she wasn't a dream? You were hallucinating. A lot."

I hesitated, not wanting to sound crazy—but I had a suspicion, and I thought that the Princess would be as close to a safe person to ask as any I was likely to find here. "I think I saw her that time in the bazaar—when we were coming from the mundane world."

The Princess frowned and then said, "What did she smell like?"

I opened my mouth to say that was a weird question,

but as I did I remembered the incense and books smell she'd distinctly had—and said so.

The Princess nodded. "It's the High Priestess."

"Arcana," I swore.

The Princess gave me her quirk of a smile. "She likes being mysterious and enjoys her secrets." The smile faded and she seemed suddenly uncomfortable. We sat in silence for a moment, marshaling our own thoughts.

"I didn't thank you coherently," I said. "Or apologize for being a pain. Thank you, Your Highness. You saved my life."

"It was more than me."

I snorted.

"You carried me out of the mundane world," I said. She watched me, reserved. I remembered thinking that she was aloof at my party when I'd first met her. Now I thought it was something like patience. I said, "I was sort of awful, too."

She seemed mildly pleased. "You're welcome, Charity. I don't know what the future holds for you. I do think any future will be better if we're friends though—for Swords and Wands."

"Sure," I said, surprised at her gravitas. Having said what I wanted to, I waited for her to explain why she'd come to see me. After a moment of silence, she said: "I hear you tried out some more Swords magic this afternoon."

"Maybe a little."

"Are you feeling up to a proper lesson?"

"The sooner, the better," I said, thinking of the Queen

of Swords' comment about Wands' casualties. I kept wondering what had been going on there in the last week. "You're going to teach me?" I asked, hopeful.

"Ah, no," said the Princess. "It'll be the Knight."

I laughed. I thought it must be a joke.

The Princess lifted the corner of her mouth, but her amusement was at me—not with me.

"He hates me," I said. "You literally had to stop him from stabbing me like, this morning."

"He wouldn't have stabbed you this morning," she said. "You're a Sword."

"See the fact that you have to say that is enough of a problem. A Sword I might be, but he's not a fan of Charity Waits," I said. She finally laughed, her lips parting to show perfect white teeth.

"No," said the Princess, "but he's the best at combative magic." She hesitated and said, "The Queen thinks that if you two have to work together, there's a chance he'll be less..."

"Homicidal?"

"Sure."

I nodded. I could appreciate the strategy, but I didn't think it was going to work. The Knight of Swords despised me and I didn't particularly like the bastard.

"Does she have a plan?" I asked, feeling like even a really good plan wasn't going to have much chance against the Queen of Wands.

"The beginning of one," said the Princess. She sighed, and seemed ready to come to a point. "So, my Queen... she mentioned that you didn't have the full story about your father and the former Princess of Swords."

I turned to stare at her, the sentence taking a solid moment to hit me fully.

"What?" I asked.

"The Queen also said you got your focus. Before you were expelled from the House of Wands."

"I did," I said.

"Then I can tell you how I got mine."

Oh...

"You saw her die," I said, swallowing hard.

THIRTEEN

Momento Mori

THE PRINCESS OF SWORDS FIDDLED with the papers she'd brought with her. They looked like they might have been letters.

"You... was my father there?" I asked.

"Yes," she said, watching me carefully.

I didn't want to know and I needed to know at the same time.

"What..." I swallowed again, the words sticking in me.

She nodded, as though I'd been able to properly ask the question.

"It was spring and they were in a garden outside the Palace of Wands. There were tulips, red and yellow and orange—whole banks of them. The Princess of Swords went there to try to save him. She knew she was walking into a trap, that the Queen of Wands knew about them." She waited for me to say something, expectant.

Them?

I didn't get it.

"He was going to run away with the Princess of Swords. To us," she said.

My head spun.

"Oh f— He was in love with her? My fucking father was in love with the Princess of Swords and that's what— oh World damn it all! Fucking—" I got up to pace, marching back and forth across the room. I kicked the wall with the ball of my foot, thudding into the plaster. The Princess of Swords watched me with a raised eyebrow.

"You're kidding?" I said, finally. Not because I thought she was or didn't believe her, but because I hoped against hope that it was a fucking joke.

She shook her head.

"Do you believe me?"

I kept pacing and tried to think through the anger. I knew that the Queen of Wands, my mother, had killed my father. She'd admitted it, at a moment when she was sure I about to be dead too. She let me go to the mundane world because she couldn't stand the sight of me... because I looked like him. I'd always known the Princess of Swords died at the same time my father did. Now I knew how their deaths were connected.

"You saw him die?" I asked.

"No," she said. "I— she died first. But he was— the Queen had beaten him. He was addled too. Like he'd been hit with a spell."

I remembered the way the Ten had knocked me out before my mother came to kill me.

"I bet he was," I whispered.

"The Queen of Wands fought briefly with my predecessor, but my Princess... she was good, but the Queen of Wands is exceptionally powerful, even for a Court Card."

"Did you... you saw the whatever it is— the memory of this moment when you got your focus—you saw it through the Princess's eyes?"

"Of course," said the Princess of Swords.

"Not... so you actually *died as her*?"

"Yes. Didn't you? Die as the Princess of Wands?"

"I saw the Princess of Wands die, but it was through my mother's eyes. The Queen of Wands."

The Princess frowned. "Really? That's not usual."

I laughed. "Of course it isn't. Nothing's bloody usual about me." I turned to her, and said. "Did my father— what was he like? In that moment?"

She flinched. "Charity, I understand wanting to know..." she caught my eye, and said: "He was a mess. He pled with her, and she made him watch the Princess die first."

We were silent for a few minutes after that. I was chasing my own thoughts in circles and she tapped a finger on the papers she'd brought with her.

She set them on the desk. "These are from your father, to her," she said. "I inherited them when I became the Princess of Swords. I thought you might want them."

I glared at the letters, but nodded. Speaking seemed inordinately difficult.

"I'll tell the Knight," said the Princess, "That you're ready for a lesson tomorrow. I'll be there to make sure he doesn't get out of hand."

I nodded.

"Get some rest if you can. You've got a lot more to do."

"Oh good," I snapped. She nodded to herself and got up, when she was at the door and about to leave I drew in a breath and said: "Thank you."

I hoped she wouldn't ask me exactly what I was thanking her for. It would have been hard to try to put into words at the moment.

However, all the Princess did was nod, and then she left me alone.

FOURTEEN

Airing The Issues

I DIDN'T LOOK AT THE LETTERS that night. I couldn't bring myself to do it.

Sure that I wouldn't sleep, I went to bed furious. My body, however, had other ideas. I was still recovering and I'd tired myself out practicing air magic. I fell asleep almost immediately. When I woke up, I was well rested— and still angry.

Before I had the chance to work myself up to those letters, the Princess of Swords sent Camilla to collect me for my lesson with the Knight of Swords. Nursing my bad mood, I trailed her blue and white livery through the corridors and across the sky bridges of the Palace.

My destination was an enormous atrium. Around me, balconies rose to five or six stories. Each railing was awash in flowers, so that a cascade—a waterfall—of blooms washed down the sides of the space. A smaller, literal waterfall burbled at one end of the room and the rest of the space was clear. The air was warm and humid, but not unpleasantly so, and somehow they were letting in real sunlight—though I couldn't see the windows, or how they'd contrived it, since we were somewhere in the middle of the tower.

As I had many times, I reminded myself that this was the City—the whole place was improbable at best, and impossible the rest of the time.

The room reminded me of one of the King of Wands' biodomes, making me feel surprisingly homesick. I hoped he was alright, that he was finding ways to fight my mother's hooks in him. I thought about dancing with him at my party. It seemed like forever ago. I wished my Path could have stayed as simple as it seemed before my mother returned.

Off to the side of the atrium, there were a few pieces of training equipment—a dummy, some mats and a few wooden swords.

I walked up and down the tiled floor, peering up and enjoying the flowers. I was in a better mood by the time the Knight and Princess arrived. It didn't last long.

"Let's begin," the Knight said, without preamble. The Princess passed me, on her way to a staircase that would put her on a balcony above us. She touched my shoulder as she went and whispered, "Good luck."

I took a breath. I was determined to hold onto my temper. I wanted to show the Knight that even as a new part of the House of Swords, I was going to take it seriously.

He stood opposite me. "We'll start with breathing exercises," he said.

The next hour was all about controlling my breath. It started to feel very silly. I didn't know that I could make my lungs sore from constantly filling them to their fullest, but apparently I could.

When the Knight of Swords was apparently satisfied that I'd learned to breathe properly, he said, "Hold out your hand now, like so." He put out a hand, palm towards me and I mirrored him. It wasn't all that different from the pose that I had used when I was channeling fire.

"Now," he said. "When I say 'go', channel your breath through your hand in a solid push. Go!" He shouted the last word, surprising me. He threw air magic at me, and I felt like I was struck by a large heavy balloon. I flew backwards, landing on my ass and sliding across the tile.

"What the *fuck*?" I said with feeling. I stood up, and touched my tailbone, feeling where the bruise would be.

"You'll need to be faster than that," he said.

"You're supposed to be teaching me," I said. I fought the urge to glance up to the Princess of Swords.

"I am," he said. He brought his hand back up. "Ready?"

I brought my hand up fast as he said: "Go!"

I was more prepared for it, this time. I was able to roll away from him and didn't land so hard.

I snarled as I came back up with my hand ready. So much for not losing my temper. As with fire, I could hold more power when I was angry.

He smiled, cold and unconcerned. I wavered between the desire to try for a good impression with the Princess and the desire to break his fucking nose.

He lazily put his hand up, and I tried to remember my breathing or anything even remotely like the magic I had been learning. I tried to counter him, but he blew my shield of air apart.

I took another tumble and landed close to the mats. That we weren't using.

I took a deep breath and didn't bounce back up. I held my arm as though I'd hurt it.

"Get up," he said, not the least curious or sympathetic.

"Charity?" called the Princess from the balcony.

I took an extra beat, pretending that pulling myself together was harder than it actually was. I focused on my breath and on my hand.

When I stood facing him, I raised my hand again. He sneered and raised his hand, saying 'go' as he did so.

I released a breath and pushed with all my might.

I have no illusions. If he'd been ready for me, I never would have thrown him so far. He, however, wasn't ready for me. He underestimated the hell out of me. I sent him up into the air and he hit the plants and the first floor balcony with a crunch that made me flinch. He fell down to the tile floor and I was worried for half a second that I was about to be in a lot of trouble. He managed to use some air to slow down his fall at the last minute and landed on one knee. In my head, I heard Delia say, *"oh kitten"* and saw the way she'd shake her head at me losing my temper like that.

I stood for an instant, listening to the gentle burble of the waterfall, waiting.

He stood up, slowly, and looked at me with malevolence. I could see, out of the corner of my eye, the Princess of Swords holding her face with one hand. I shrugged and didn't apologize.

He stepped up to me and put up his hand.

"Go."

FIFTEEN

In My Father's Words

I FINISHED MY FIRST LESSON with the Knight of Swords with a record number of bruises and a stubborn pride in how I'd acquitted myself. The Princess of Swords watched the whole lesson, and each time I saw her edge towards the staircase or seem like she was about to intervene, I would throw my own thinly veiled insult at the Knight. She would stop, raise her eyebrows or shake her head, and resume her watch over us without intervening.

While it might not have been the smartest thing I ever did, the lesson certainly kept me from thinking about anything else. There was something refreshing about throwing all my strength against someone I couldn't hurt. It felt good to ache in a way that had to do with exercise and not my magic. I felt properly alive for the first time since I'd been exiled from the House of Wands.

My father's letters, though, were waiting for me when I limped back to my room.

I was standing in the middle of the room, staring at them, when someone knocked at the door.

"Yes?" I said. Camilla ducked her head in.

"The—uh, Princess sent you..." she trailed off, and held out a card.

I moved over and took it. It was a tarot card—a four of swords. It showed a woman on her bed, leaning back on the wall behind her and propped up with a sword—using the weapon like a cane, with the point stuck in the floor below. The other three swords were scattered at her feet. The window over her head was made of stained glass. It was a card for rest and for healing.

"Thank you very much," I said. Camilla nodded and closed the door. I heard it lock.

It was a small thing, a card to help me deal with the beating I'd taken, but it showed some trust to give me even one card. They all knew what I'd managed with just a two of swords.

I sat on my bed with the card and focused on healing myself with it. It wasn't magic I'd practiced and I was already tired, but it helped.

After cleaning myself up, I stood staring at the damn letters again.

They weren't going to go away. I should either read them or give them back to the Princess of Swords—not let them sit there and torture me.

I picked them up. The paper was thin and fragile. It was my father's handwriting. I started to open them up, unfolding each in order and laying them first on the desk and then on the floor around the desk. It gave me one last excuse to avoid reading them.

I couldn't help but think they might be forged. The Swords might be hoping to further manipulate me. What could they do with a sample of my father's writing and magic?

I didn't like how paranoid that felt. It sounded like my mother's voice.

As in the atrium with the Knight, I imagined Delia here. She'd be looking from me to the letters, worried and letting me take my time with them. It would have been nice to have her support. Alphonso would have walked right across all the old paper—that sounded nice too.

I started to read the letters.

My memories of the City before I left are fuzzy and limited. I didn't remember my parents together much. I remembered my father fairly clearly, but I remembered playing with him, or watching him work—building something using cards. These letters though were something different from that memory. They formed a peculiar version of my father. I wasn't so young when he died, but in reading his words I saw that my idea was so terribly partial that it did him no justice. The man in these letters bore no resemblance to my father. They described someone called Henry Waits. He was bitterly unhappy, mortally resentful of his Queen, and in love with the Princess of Swords.

The letters started out friendly—a casual correspondence on magic and building and their social lives—commentary on the differences between Wands and Swords. Then they become more intense, more specific, and more aspirational.

"... Forgive me, if my sentiments are too simple. I wish that I had more complex terms to put them in, but I have never been simply in love before. It is that simplicity I treasure. You may doubt me, but I promise that beside the complicated and twisting alleys where once I found something that passed for affection, the clear and open path of our mutual desire is more revitalizing to me than all the mazes a more intricate seduction might offer..."

I skimmed through the next few. I couldn't quite think of the person in the letters as my father. It was disconcerting to see him as a lovestruck man, seven years dead.

I wondered what had happened to her letters responding. Surely my mother had burned them all, if she found them. He made reference to the Princess's comments and answered questions I had to guess at.

Once, I thought she must have asked why—if he felt the way he professed to—he didn't declare it to the City. It must have been something like that, because he answered:

"...I don't know where to begin. She does not love me, does not even think of me— but believe me, if I were to openly love another, if I were to have a life beyond her, beyond her daughter and beyond the House of Wands, then she would think of me. She would command me to end it. Though it would destroy me to lose our correspondence, I understand if risking the wroth of the Queen of Wands is too much for you..."

The reference to 'her' daughter hurt. Not 'his' or 'our'. Her daughter. I was surprised to see how well he understood my mother though—I'd always thought of him as somehow ignorant of her personality, deceived the way it seemed the Knight of Wands was. Of course, in retrospect that was unlikely. He might have been in the beginning, but he almost must have learned better when they separated.

I kept reading, and my heart skipped a beat when I appeared more prominently in the letters.

I gathered from his comments that the Princess suggested he come to the Palace of Swords, if he was so afraid of the Queen of Wands.

"...You haven't met Charity, I know, and it is true that in many ways she takes after her mother—in her strength and her temper. I cannot leave her behind. I won't concede her to her mother. The Queen has ambitions for Charity—and I fear what she could become, left solely in her mother's grasp..."

I put down the letter. Then I moved away from them.

I was absurdly angry at him for not acting quickly enough. I was angry too that—having understood so much about my mother—he hadn't seen the danger more clearly. And I missed him. Surely our parents are as lost as we are—but it would have been comforting to have someone I could pretend would take care of me.

When I was ready, as much recovered as I thought I was going to get, I skimmed through the last few letters, brushing aside errant tears in irritation.

I almost missed the line that said, a few letters later:

"...Tomorrow, I will tell Charity that we are leaving the Palace of Wands..."

What?

I didn't remember that.

I read the line again, and then the surrounding passages. My father was sure of my unhappiness in the Palace of Wands. We were going to escape, and damn the consequences. No complication was too much for their love.

I stared at the words and reread them again.

He never got to tell me. Whatever had gone wrong had happened before he did.

The final letter was different. It read, in its entirety:

"My love —

I long so to see you. I know it's complicated. I'll see you alone under the trees where we first met. The tulips are all in bloom there now.

Until we meet again.

Henry"

I felt sick. It was the same handwriting, but nothing at all like the other letters. He'd reminisced several times about how he'd met the Princess of Swords—none of that mentioned trees.

It was a warning or a trap. Or both. It had to be. She must have known, reading that note, that their plan was discovered. She hadn't stayed away.

So. My father loved the Princess of Swords. He'd

risked everything, foolishly, infuriatingly and under-standably for that. I thought that she must have loved him too. Or she wouldn't have gone to try to save him.

There was only one person, of course, who would have set the trap. My mother. I knew my father was right—even if she hadn't loved him, she would have wanted to control him in the same way that, though she didn't care for me, she'd wanted my obedience. Plotting to escape to the House of Swords would have been unac-ceptable to her. Taking me with him would have been an issue too—I didn't know how big of one, but definitely a problem for her.

I carefully refolded the letters. Perhaps it was better that I had no fire.

I caught a whiff of incense and heard a faint chuckle, somewhere behind my ear. I turned fast, but I was alone in the room. As alone as one gets on the Fool's Path. The High Priestess is the keeper of secrets—seemed that dig-ging through these letters, this history, pleased her.

You can't see me.

I heard her voice in my head, and I was uncertain whether it was her presence or my own memory.

SIXTEEN

Edges of Air

DESPITE USING THE FOUR OF SWORDS to heal myself, I was still sore and achy when I got up the next day. I grumbled through it, stretching in spite of myself. I'd put my father's letters in a drawer, out of sight, and found that even so I avoided looking at the desk itself—like that would mean I didn't have to think about their implications.

My next lessons in the House of Swords went much like the first. I practiced summoning air and got faster. The Knight didn't pull his punches, but he had to work harder to throw me sideways. We started using the mats after the first lesson. He said that it was important to know what it felt like to hit a real floor. I suspected, however, after a few more lessons, that he felt somewhat guilty for the way he'd behaved. He was rude and cold, but he didn't sneer the way he had the first day.

The Princess stuck her head in to check on us sometimes, keeping an eye on the Knight and my progress. I wasn't sure if she was monitoring my skills or our relationship. Or both.

Once, Hector came to see how I was doing too. He strolled in, deliberately casual, while the Knight and I were taking a breather. His sudden appearance gave me the visceral feeling that we were back in the Magus's house. For a moment I expected the room to transform and the vines hanging from the balconies to try to strangle us all. Strange, that I was safer in the Palace of Swords than I'd ever been in the Magus's house.

"Hello," Hector said and I waved to him. He glanced at the Knight, who did not acknowledge him, before letting out a little sigh and focusing on me. "How are you, Charity?"

"I've been better," I said, honestly. "But at least he's not trying to kill me." I joked about that a lot. It was my way of coping. And it seemed to annoy the Knight—he snorted, anyway.

Hector almost smiled, but the expression didn't quite make it to his lips.

"What about you?" I asked.

Hector shrugged. "I'll be leaving to spend some time with Justice soon. The Princess says it's only a matter of time before the Arcana sends for me. I'm ready, apparently."

"Are you?" asked the Knight. It sounded like he was trying, but couldn't quite manage, to keep the spite from his voice.

"You could judge for yourself," Hector pointed out, coolly.

The Knight nodded. "I haven't seen your constructs," he said. He stood up and I staggered to my feet with him. "Show me," he continued. "Miss Waits can use all the practice she can get."

The Knight backed up, arms crossed, to give us space. He watched critically while Hector drew a few of his disposable twos of swords and looked at me with some concern. "I'll be careful," he promised. I nodded. I trusted Hector—with my life, actually.

Hector summoned two constructs—one flying on wings of air and the other a spindly humanoid shape. They attacked at the same time. I threw a lash of air at the spindly one—trying to find the card at its heart—and ducked under the diving construct.

I wished, briefly, that I had my fire back. It wasn't stronger or anything, just more familiar.

I met the spindly construct's punches with a shield of air, forcing it back, and countered with knives of air that I couldn't quite make sharp enough to cut Hector's cards.

We sparred like that—Hector staying away from me and managing to counter my attempts to distract him from holding the constructs by attacking him directly too. After ten minutes or so of back and forth, we both withdrew. I was out of breath and chuckling.

I expected the Knight of Swords to be irritated that we hadn't been more aggressive in our contest, but he was nodding to himself when we stopped. He directed his comment to Hector, without facing him fully.

"You improved."

Hector gave a little bow.

"We're done for the day," the Knight said to me. "You need to practice making an edge." I rolled my eyes and turned to Hector, hoping he would come and have dinner with me. I hadn't had a chance to talk to him about the letters from my father—and it would be nice not to be alone. It was not to be, however.

"Hector, stay a minute?" asked the Knight. "I have a few suggestions."

Hector nodded. "Of course," he said.

I remembered the Knight's angry words when he'd discovered I'd become a Sword and Hector describing the Knight as his friend. I lingered for a moment, intensely curious about what they had to say to each other. When I didn't move, the Knight turned his glare on me.

"Go," he snapped. I suppose I should be grateful he didn't throw me out of the room with magic.

Camilla was waiting for me. She walked me back to my room, and I was left to wonder what the Knight and Hector talked about.

SEVENTEEN

The Bodies

AFTER A DIFFERENT LESSON, I was back in my room and standing in front of my closet, considering the odd variety of Swords clothing available to me. I'd taken to, in private, talking to Delia when I was by myself. I kept trying to think of a way to let her know I was alive, and trying to argue myself into the idea that she could keep the secret— but it hadn't worked yet. My father's letters were yet another reminder not to underestimate my mother's vindictive tendencies—not that I needed it. Delia was safest thinking I was dead.

"Right, Dee," I said to no one. "Which do you think?" I was contemplating trying one of the fancier outfits, just for the change of pace. Someone knocked on my door and opened it at my call.

I realized, when they did, that it wasn't locked. I felt an absurd surge of accomplishment before the serious face of a servant appeared. It was the Queen's sword bearer.

"Her Majesty wants you," he rumbled, without preamble. "Now."

"I'll be ready in a minute," I said.

"I'm to wait," he said.

I nodded, and grabbed a formal jacket. It overlapped in the front—closing with silk frogs on the side—and was made from a dramatic blue and white geometric print. It was cinched with a wide black belt stamped with a pattern of feathers and swords in silver.

I dressed in the bathroom and returned to follow the sword bearer. He took me to the elevators and we went up.

We stepped out into a huge formal lobby—the kind you would find in a grand old playhouse—and we hurried straight through a set of double doors and into the Swords' throne room.

It was built like a large theater, but without chairs or a proscenium arch. There was a balcony, and as I came out from under it, I could see the front of the space without obstruction. Four silver thrones sat beneath nine boxes— like small private theater boxes, but facing the audience. Over the balconies were fourteen rose windows, each representing one of the cards in the Suit of Swords. High around the edge of the room were more rose windows, each unique, and surely pulled from different cathedrals in the mundane world. Light poured through them, bathing the room in rainbows.

The Court of Swords was present, all four of them. Behind them were several Swords I didn't recognize—I thought they must be numbered cards. I scanned the faces for Hector, but didn't see him.

The Court stood over three bodies, which rested on blood-stained white sheets, laid out in a funereal manner. The King stood apart, fingers pinching the bridge of his nose.

I slowed down, seeing the corpses, hoping that I wouldn't recognize any of them.

Upon closer inspection, they seemed to be Sword guards. They were certainly dead—one from a head wound and one from a blow to the chest. The chest wound was an odd shape, the hole in the body resembled an eight pointed star. There were scorch marks on both impact sites. I felt a mortifying mix of relief and horror.

Wands.

"Charity," said the Queen. "Good. We'd like your opinion on something."

I swallowed. I wasn't sure what I could offer here.

"What happened?" I asked.

"What do you think?" asked the Knight, acidly.

I didn't turn to him. My jaw twitched and I waited for the Queen to reply.

She sighed, hunched over and leaning on her cane. "There was a confrontation—this one in our territory. Near the de facto border with Wands, true, but where we would have thought our people were safe."

"I'm sorry," I said, dying to ask if there had been any Wands hurt—and who was there.

The Knight snorted. I wanted to throw a fucking fireball at him.

"The Seven of Wands was there—we didn't get him," she said.

I kept my face carefully blank.

"You wanted my opinion on something," I said, mouth dry.

"Yes," said the Queen, she thumped her stick on the floor. "The Queen of Wands announced this morning, publicly, that you'd been captured and likely murdered by us—the House of Swords. I want to know if you know how she could have found out."

Everyone in the room was staring at me, and my mind had gone completely and fiercely blank with panic.

EIGHTEEN

My Mother's Mind

I CLOSED MY MOUTH, WHICH had fallen open and glanced at the Princess of Swords. She was watching me closely, aloof. I could guess what the Knight looked like, and didn't bother to glance his way.

I racked my brain for how she could possibly have known where I was. Or that I was alive. I tried not to think of Delia.

"Someone could have seen me? Coming back from the Eiffel Tower?" I threw out the idea, not at all convinced myself.

"From where?" asked the Queen.

"The tower," I said. "The one we used to move between the mundane world and the City."

The Princess of Swords shook her head, slowly. "I had us strongly warded," she said. "I would have noticed, if someone saw us."

"A finding spell?" I asked, like the ones I'd used to find my mother or Delia. *Oh World, let her be safe.*

"Our defenses are built to withstand that sort of thing," said the Queen.

"How do you think we've kept her away from the Princess of Swords?" sneered the Knight.

"Spies in the Palace here?" I asked, ignoring him.

"One particular spy, perhaps," said the Knight.

"You've been kept rather a careful secret," said the Queen, also ignoring him. I opened my mouth to protest, but it was true that I'd seen very few people in the Palace since I'd been here. There was no one else in the corridors or elevators coming here, for example, or when I'd gone to my lessons with the Knight.

"Camilla?" I asked.

"My granddaughter?" said the Queen of Swords.

Oh.

"Have you no defense besides blaming others?" asked the Knight.

I finally turned to him. "How the fuck am I supposed to have talked to her, exactly?"

"I don't know," he snapped. "She's reputed to be clever, your mother. Perhaps the point has been this, all along."

I shook my head, angry and trying to remember where I'd heard something like that before.

It took me a minute. I stared up at the windows, at the central one that depicted the Ace of Swords.

"No..." I said slowly, remembering.

Before my presentation party the King of Wands and I had spoken about the Queen of Wands. I'd thought she was dead then, and I'd said something about how she'd wanted me to hate the City and distrust everyone—I couldn't be sure what I actually thought and what it was she wanted me to do or say or think. The King had said:

Even your mother was not as complicated as you are making her. You give her credit for all her intentions manifesting in the way she conceived them. That isn't true for anyone.

I sent the King a quick thank you in my head, and included his health in my silent prayers to the World for Delia's sake. I hoped he was alright, and I got a chance to thank him for that insight.

"She's lying," I said. That solution made more sense the more I thought about it. I started talking quickly, "She doesn't know I'm here. She just said it because it gets the House of Wands riled up against you. It's an easy explanation—all she has to say is that you lot caught me outside the Magus's house. It's believable after my run in with your guards." *And Delia must have told them about Hector,* I thought, but I didn't say it out loud— in case it got Hector in more trouble.

"She got lucky," I concluded. "But it's a shot in the dark."

The Queen of Swords pursed her lips and then let out a high humorless cackle.

The Knight threw up his hands. "We're supposed to trust that?"

"Yes," I said, pressing the point—more certain by the second. "She's good at this—she'll find a way to turn anything to her advantage. She didn't want me back in the City in the first place, but she took credit for it—to the House and with me when she wanted me on her side. She doesn't know where I am—it's merely convenient if Wands think you have me. If you deny it, the Wands won't believe it. I'm sure she doesn't think you have me, but if I were to appear over here, she'd still be able to use the fact to motivate the House. And if she can find me and kill me, she'll show them my body—and already have planted the idea that you are to blame."

"World damn that woman's luck," said the Queen of Swords. "Even when she doesn't know what's going on she manages to be a thorn in my side."

"You don't believe her?" said the Knight, incredulous.

"Can you think of a better explanation?" I snapped at him. "You know the bloody Queen of Wands."

He crossed his arms, glaring at me.

The Princess of Swords was gazing off into the distance, also considering something. I wished I knew what she was thinking—I was starting to distinguish between the two sides to her. This aloof persona and the more relaxed and friendly version I'd seen occasionally.

"I think Charity is right," said the Princess, now, her tone thoughtful. She looked to the King of Swords. He still focused on the bodies, frowning, but he gave a short nod.

"I'm inclined to agree," said the Queen of Swords. "I think it's likely, even." She turned to me. "The announcement escalated the fighting in the streets. There have been injuries, in the last few days—these deaths are the first. There will be more. How're the lessons going?"

"Great," said the Knight and I in unison and with the same sarcastic tone. We both flinched and then glared at each other.

"Good," said the Queen, glancing between us with a knowing eye. "Keep working. And get her a deck. It's time."

NINETEEN

Pick A Card...

I SAT ON BED WITH MY NEW tarot cards, relieved and surprised by how much better having a deck felt.

With the benefit of hindsight, I'll say I was not always the most responsible when it came to learning about my tarot deck. Frankly, it took losing my beautiful living deck for me to better appreciate its power and what it offered. Now, armed with a common deck, I set to studying the thing—practicing pulling a handful of cards that I knew how to use in combat.

A few seemed to work better for me. The seven of wands came easily—this deck showing a woman, holding steady against six invisible opponents. So too, did the five of wands—which showed an unruly brawl between five children with clubs. They appeared to be laughing, and it felt like a game that would remain fun right up until someone got a proper whack from one of those clubs.

To my surprise, I drew the princess of swords and found that the art must be a few years old. The woman on the card looked a lot like the Knight of Swords—the deck must have been made when his sister was the Princess. That one felt good in my hand, and while I didn't want to experiment too much with it in the limited space of my room, I thought that combining it with my air magic might let me make something similar to the wind knives I'd seen the Knight of Swords conjure. The Knight might think it was a shortcut, but given the situation I didn't feel bad about that at all. I'll admit that the daydream of using the princess of swords against my mother had a feeling of justice to it. I wondered what my father would have thought of it.

Despite my better judgement, I tried using the ace of wands. The card showed a great tree branch, bearing flowers made of fire. After struggling with it, I managed to summon a tiny flame—smaller than even a cigarette lighter would have given me. I sighed. I'd never used the ace to summon fire before. I'd never needed to. I tried not to be irritated that it didn't come more naturally to me. After all, I wasn't a part of the House of Wands anymore.

I worked well into the night, practicing with the deck and learning my new cards.

It must have been close to midnight when I started to draw the High Priestess.

The card showed a seated woman with a curtain of wavy black hair on either side of her oval face. Her pallor was sky blue, her gown black with white showing in the heart of its pleats. Behind her was a star-strewn curtain—concealing the mysteries she guarded. I looked at the card, and it made me feel mildly uncomfortable—a slight repulsion emanated from it. I put it back in the deck and tried to draw the seven of wands.

I drew the High Priestess again.

I stared at her, feeling the beginning of worry. I put the card back, sliding it into the middle of the stack, and set the deck down in front of me on the bedspread.

I stared at it for a minute, like facing down a stray dog—waiting to see if it was going to bite or not. I flipped over the top card of the deck.

It was the High Priestess.

Right.

She had my attention. I'd been sitting cross-legged on the bed, and now I pushed myself up to a more dignified kneeling position. I set the card in front of me and rested my hands on my knees.

I focused, tried to clear my mind and thought about the High Priestess.

I knew that I had her attention when the light went out.

I sat very still, blinking and willing my eyes to adjust to the sudden darkness.

When I started to see what was around me though, it wasn't my room anymore—I couldn't see the glow of the City from around the edges of the black curtain covering my giant window. I was kneeling on a thin rug—not my bed. I saw the outline of a door and a hallway beyond. It didn't match up with the door to my room, the closet, or the bathroom.

"Hello?" I said, and I could smell the incense wafting from the doorway. The walls were blue and decorated with raised geometric patterns—alternating intricate ten and twelve pointed stars with woven centers.

"A passage, a card, a broken dream," sang the High Priestess. "Fire and air and blisters."

I stood up, carefully.

"Arcana?" I asked.

"Fool," she said, "You can't *see* me."

"No, I can't, Arcana. Where are you?"

She chuckled. "I'm here, my dear. You just can't see me."

I glanced around, peering into the shadows. I didn't see even her vague veiled form.

"Where?" I asked.

"Right in front of you."

She definitely wasn't there.

I heard her chuckle and sigh again. "Go look," she said. "Go look. You'll see."

TWENTY

Fate Unsealed

MY LEGS WERE STIFF AND mostly asleep from kneeling. With an effort, I unfolded them. The mundane prickle of pins and needles in my legs contrasted with the ethereal hallway.

I stood in front of it, flexing my feet. The incense was thicker in the air here, almost overwhelmingly sweet— and under it the dusty smell of old books again. I breathed shallowly through my mouth. I felt the same repulsion I'd felt from the High Priestess card when I'd drawn it. Why couldn't the Arcana just come and have a nice straight-forward chat?

I stepped over the threshold and started hearing voices. Dozens and dozens of women's voices, muffled by the blue walls around me. They were chattering and laughing and whispering, quietly enough that I couldn't pick out any single sentence or follow any thought properly.

I took a breath of the incense filled air and started forward. The floor beneath my bare feet was ceramic tile—painted in patterns of blue, with yellow details.

The voices rose and fell around me. At the end of the hallway, I could see a curtain—the same sort that had been in her card—dark blue and embroidered with stars and pomegranates.

A few steps brought me to the curtain.

She likes her mysteries.

All the Major Arcana are dangerous—some in oblivious ways and some deceptively. The High Priestess had said 'go look', peek behind the curtain—but I was afraid. The sweet incense made my head swim.

What test or task did the High Priestess have for me here?

The fabric was heavy and soft under my fingers, and I pulled it back.

The walls beyond were stone—tiled in black and orange. There wasn't a light source—it should have been pitch black—but the bluish glow from the hallway lingered here too, faint but enough to illuminate the square space. A dozen tables of different shapes and sizes were set in the room with enough to walk between them.

On the tables were tarot cards.

The cards were laid out in patterns and connected with lines of paint or chalk. I bent down to examine one on a large table by the entrance to the room.

It must have been made by combining a dozen different decks, because it created a circular pattern alternating only fours of swords with eights of swords. The four I knew from when the Ten and my mother had trapped me—and again from when the Princess had given it to me to help me heal from my training with the Knight of Swords. All the art was different, but each version of the card showed sleeping figures.

The eights of swords were more ominous. Each showed a figure standing blindfolded and bound from head to foot in the midst of a forest of swords—sharp edges all around them.

At the center of the pattern was the King of Wands, enthroned and gazing out of his card at me. Crossing him—half covering him and holding him down was the Hanged Man, one of the Major Arcana. The Hanged Man is strung up over a chasm. He can't move or escape or change. He is suspended, isolated from the world around him.

My gut caught up with what this was before I did. It was the spell—the seal—that my mother was using to keep the King of Wands under her control.

I put out a hand to take away the Hanged Man and set the King free.

I couldn't pick up the card. My hand passed over it, but I couldn't move it or disturb the pattern. I wasn't really here.

Swallowing, I took in the rest of the room. There were at least a dozen tables with cards on them and half a dozen empty ones. What the hell was she doing with all of this?

I walked through the room, looking down at the different patterns, feeling all the power that was tied up here.

At the back of the room, on a small, low table, I found the spell I'd been sent to find—without knowing what it was I was searching for.

On one side were two cards, crossed at an angle to make an 'X'. The one on top was the ten of cups. It looked almost like a family portrait—showing a loving couple holding each other and sitting under a tree, while a little girl played nearby, stacking the cups that named the card in a small pyramid. Under that was the princess of wands. I couldn't see her properly, couldn't move the card to see her—but a chill ran through me seeing this. Surrounding those two cards was a square made of eight more bound and blindfolded eights of swords—and faraway, removed from the rest of the cards was the High Priestess—set over a second card. One I couldn't see.

Dust covered all these cards in a thick and undisturbed layer.

"I can't see you," I said, finally understanding. I felt a kind of contented sigh from the presence of the High Priestess, relief and approval from her as I solved a mystery.

This was a spell to keep a secret from me—to hide something. My mother was using the High Priestess against me, keeping me in the dark.

I knew it wouldn't work, but I tried to lift the High Priestess and see what was under it. My fingers slid frustratingly over the card without being able to touch it, leaving the dust undisturbed.

I looked up and faced the High Priestess.

She stood with the low table between us, having brought me here. Her face was turned down and way from me, shielded by her hair and diaphanous veils. She ran a hand through the dust, passing her fingers over her card and back again. Each of her fingers bore a ring, her hand was heavy with silver and bronze. At the first pass she left no mark. The second time though, the second time her fingers left a trail behind them— two thin lines through the dust.

I jerked my eyes up to her face, shaking without knowing why.

"Lies," she sang, "secrets, choking dust, and time past." She stared back at me. "She should have known it couldn't last."

The High Priestess pressed down on her own card with one finger. It lit up with the faint blue of her hallway. Her place in the City.

"Time to see me," she said and picked up the card.

TWENTY-ONE

Be Careful What You Wish For

I SAW TRIPLE WHEN THE High Priestess picked up the card, my vision blurring and splitting into three distinct sights.

The first remained the room with all my mother's seals. When the High Priestess removed her card from my seal I felt a burst of power escape, like a bubble popping. The dust flew off the cards. I felt the spell lift off of me, and I knew that I'd carried my mother's seal for so long, had been so used to it that the lightness, the freedom was strange. Under the card the High Priestess lifted, revealed, was the nine of swords. A central figure crouched on the ground, holding their knees with their head bowed, under the shadow of nine swords.

The second sight was the High Priestess herself. She grew in my vision, rising up and past the ceiling of the small room. She towered over me and her veil shredded away to nothing. She was a swirl of stars and all the secrets of the City lived in her eyes. Those densely packed secrets threatened to pull me in—her eyes had their own gravity. I knew, as clearly as I knew my name, that people had drowned here—faced with all that hidden knowledge.

The third sight was the secret—the one that threatened to drown me.

My father had told me we were leaving, escaping to the House of Swords.

I'd told my mother.

I remembered now. He came to me, sitting on the end of my bed in a room I'd forgotten until this moment. I'd forgotten so so much.

"We need to talk," he'd said. *Oh World, I did look like him.* We had the same green eyes and brown hair. The same nose. I recognized in me the way he moved his hand, touching his forehead to buy himself time to figure out what to say. How to say this.

"Charity, I know you're unhappy here."

How wary I'd been that this was a trap. I couldn't be unhappy. I was the daughter of the Queen of Wands, and I was going to be the most powerful sorcerer the City had seen. I was going to be a Court Card at the least, and maybe even become a Major Arcana. The City was mine to take. That's what my mother said. But what she meant was that I was a tool. Her tool, forever. I would serve her or else. Fourteen and I knew that's what she really meant.

I shook my head, afraid.

"I'm very happy," I'd said.

He looked at me, and I knew now that even though he

saw himself in my hair and eyes, he saw my mother right behind them.

"You're not," he had snapped, telling me how I felt and annoyed because he knew I was lying to him. Frustrated that I didn't *just trust him*—just agree with him. Just be his daughter and not hers.

I didn't say anything, curling in on myself. I didn't know what he wanted me to say.

"Charity," he'd said, trying to be patient. "We're leaving. You and I. It will be better for us. For you. It's time to leave the House of Wands. You'll be happier somewhere new, I promise."

"Where are we going?" I asked, still suspecting some trap—some trick my mother was forcing him to play.

"Just trust me, Charity."

I didn't say anything. He'd been disappointed and then—after a struggle—controlled himself. He took my hands and said, "I know I haven't protected you, the way I should have." Regret in his eyes and his face. "I know," he whispered. "I want to make this better, Charity. I want to make it right and I want a new start for us. Will you do this for me, Charity? Give us a fresh start. A chance to try again?"

I didn't respond and he let me go, despairing of getting through to me.

He'd stood up and said, "You'll see. You'll understand later. I promise."

"Where are we going?" I asked again.

"Just be ready. Get anything you need to take with you ready to go. Just trust me."

My anger, slower to show back then, boiled over in a

quick hot burst and I'd yelled, "How can you say 'just trust me' when you won't even tell me where you're going?"

I'd been afraid as soon as I yelled at him, curling in on myself and waiting for retaliation.

He'd been angry too in that moment, and then controlled himself again.

"The House of Swords," he said finally.

Fear, deeply ingrained, of leaving the Palace grounds crashed in around me, compounded with my dread of and prejudice against other Suits.

I still didn't say anything, frozen with terror, and he misread my silence. He nodded, like I'd grown up in that instant—like one adult to another.

"A fresh start is what we need, you and I. I promise you, this will be better."

Idiot, I thought in the present, thinking back to this moment. I'd believed, completely, that he'd been suborned by Swords—tricked. I thought I was saving him when I ran straight to my mother and told her everything. I believed...

I hated her, even then, but I thought I needed her. I trusted her to keep me safe, because she was the most powerful person I knew.

She'd told me I was right, that she'd save him and make everything better. I was just to play along.

She'd killed him and the Princess of Swords two days later—and I tried to kill her when I realized what had happened.

It was the first time I'd pulled magic through my anger—raw betrayal and fury combining to throw itself at her, determined to burn her to a cinder for her treachery.

It had burned open a channel for my magic, one I'd stuck to until very recently.

We'd fought—flinging flames at one another until she wore me down. Not all my rage was enough to beat the Queen of Wands.

When I'd awoken, I thought Swords had killed my father. I still blamed her, still hated her—her seal wasn't powerful enough to change that. I forgot her part and mine in his death, until now. I'd left the City a month later, determined never to return.

All that flooded through me, left me lost in the High Priestess's eyes, a ghost among my mother's seals. I was weeping, remembering, when I heard the scrape of a door.

I turned around fast, towards the entrance I'd used. The High Priestess vanished. The seal was broken. I couldn't see the actual door to this room—only the blue hallway I'd arrived by—but I could see who came through it now.

My mother wore an elaborate dressing gown in gold and red, embroidered with dragons. Her golden hair hung over her shoulder in a single braid that ended near her waist.

I stumbled back into the wall of the room, fear and adrenaline and anger spiking through me like knives.

The Queen of Wands couldn't see me. She looked around the room, suspicious, her eyes sliding over me. She stepped inside, fireball in one hand. She glared into the dark corners and her eyes passed over me.

I held my breath.

She drew a card, focused on it.

I should have run, but she was between me and the door. I willed the High Priestess to guard this secret as she'd been hiding my memories.

My mother's eyes roamed over the room again—visible over the edge of the card she held—and stopped just to the left of me. Clearly, she said: "Charity."

I jumped, panicked by the sound of my name, and came abruptly awake in my bed in the Palace of Swords, with morning's light peeking around the edge of my enormous curtain.

TWENTY-TWO

Hurry Up And...

I SAT UP FAST, LOOKING AROUND my room for the High Priestess's door. It was gone, of course, as was the scent of incense. I'd fallen asleep on top of the covers—my new tarot deck scattered around me. I shot up and to the door, opening it to find Camilla.

She wasn't there.

"Camilla?" I called. Nothing. I glanced up and down the hall—the doors were all the same. I had no idea how to find anyone. I left the door and ran to get my deck and began frantically sorting through the cards, searching for any of the Court of Swords. I heard a door open and close and then, "Miss Waits?"

I spun and saw Camilla, still in her pajamas.

"I need to talk to the Court. To someone. Now," I said.

The Queen of Wands knew I wasn't dead. Fast wasn't quick enough. We needed to move now.

"Of course," she said, alarmed. "I'll go see who is awake." She trotted off down the hall. Left alone again, I thought of running—but where would I go? And what could I do on my own that wouldn't be better with the Swords? With *other* Swords. I continued to gather up my deck—counting the cards to make sure I had everything.

That calmed me down some. I opened up the curtains and looked out at the City. I wished again that I could see the Palace of Wands from my vantage point—I wasn't even sure if I was facing the right direction though.

I wasn't sure how much my mother might have figured out from the night before. That I was back in the City, probably. Maybe more.

I needed to warn Delia. She'd been safe enough if the Queen of Wands thought I was out of the picture. I glanced down at my deck, thinking about what card I might use to reach out to Delia.

Focusing on that also kept me from staggering under the weight of my rediscovered memories. They were piling up—fights with both my parents, clearer reconstructions of my mother's training and my father. Oh World, I'd gotten him killed.

I was pacing, fighting angry tears, when Camilla returned with the Princess of Swords.

"Charity," said the Princess, concerned. "I was coming to get you. You needed to see the Queen?"

"Yes," I said. "Or any of you really. Last night the High Priestess—"

The Princess put up a hand, "Tell everyone. We're meeting this morning to talk plans."

I didn't want to wait—but I nodded and closed my mouth. I followed the Princess, trying to control my anxious energy.

At first, I thought we were going back to the Swords' throne room—but we must have been in a different tower. The hallway the elevator opened on was ornately decorated with gold and silver vines on bright white plaster walls. The Princess opened the first door to our right and I found myself in what must have been the private quarters of the Queen of Swords.

The room was like a sitting room mixed with a museum. Glass cases along the walls—and some free standing—displayed weapons from a dozen different places in the mundane world, along with a handful of blades that I'm sure only ever existed in the City.

Low-backed chairs, comfortably upholstered in soft brown fabric, awaited us. Short tables between them held a selection of dainty fruits and cheeses. Already seated were the Queen and the Knight of Swords. Standing by one of the walls was the Queen's sword bearer—with her enormous focus balanced on its point in front of him.

"There you are," croaked the Queen. "Sit down—"

Before I could though, the door opened and the disheveled King of Swords stuck his head into the room. Upon seeing the group he came into the room, looking around at us in mild surprise.

"Majesty?" asked the Queen, also surprised.

"I won't keep you from your intrigue, but apparently there was a Major Arcana in the palace again last night."

Oops.

I raised a hand. "That was probably the High Priestess," I said.

The King sighed as the pieces shifted into place for him.

"You're on the Path. Of course. Forgive me, I'd forgotten."

"Sorry to be a bother," I said, and he waved a dismissive hand. He looked again at the company.

"Do I need to know?" he asked.

"It's the war with Wands," said the Queen.

The King snorted. "Win it, will you?"

"I shall endeavor to do so," said the Queen with a sharp smile. With that, the King bowed to the room and left. I'd watched this exchange with rising panic for the time we were losing.

"Sit down, Charity," said the Queen again.

"The Queen of Wands knows I'm alive," I said without preamble and without sitting.

The Queen raised her eyebrow, the Knight leaned forward and the Princess remained motionless. "So whatever plan you have—we need to do it now. Giving her time to think would be a mistake." I didn't scream: *We need to get Delia out of there!* but it was a near thing. How was I going to get word to Delia?

"Start at the beginning," commanded the Queen of Swords.

I bolted through a description of my evening with the High Priestess, the room with the seals, and the Queen of Wands. I hesitated when it came to telling them about my part in my father's death, my throat tightening painfully. I didn't want to talk about it. Or think about him. Or about what happened to him and the last Princess of Swords.

They'd know I was lying though—I didn't have anything I could reveal confidently enough to warrant the magic I was describing. Besides, I'm a terrible liar.

I told it directly to the Knight of Swords, facing him while I spoke.

His expression didn't change but under the sound of my voice a powerful stillness gathered. I would not have been surprised if he'd attacked me. I wouldn't have blamed him. Instead he stood up and moved away from the group, going to face one of the cases full of swords.

I let out a breath, pretending there weren't tears on my face. Into the silence, the Princess asked: "Did you see any seal that seemed concerned with the Knight? Or with me?"

"I'm sorry," I said. "I didn't see them all. There were plenty that could have been."

"How many were there?" she asked.

"Maybe twelve? Fourteen?"

The Queen of Swords whistled between her teeth.

"That's a lot?" I asked. I didn't know how seals worked or how much strength they required.

"That's a lot," confirmed the Queen. She narrowed her eyes. "She must have help. Even she couldn't maintain half that much. Who is helping her?"

"Could the Ten of Wands?" I asked. I couldn't think of any other Wand she would trust with that magic.

They thought about it.

"Interesting," said the Queen. "Her nature is particularly suited to assist the Queen. Perhaps it's enough."

I was nearly at the end of my patience with them, still standing over the seated Queen and Princess. I said, "So, now you know how she knows. We need to move. Fast. What's the plan?"

"You want to use Charity to draw out the Queen of Wands?" said the Princess. I was grateful for her taking up my more urgent tone.

"I do," said the Queen of Swords, with a cutting smile.

TWENTY-THREE

Furious Missteps

The Queen of Swords put it bluntly: "We need something to lure the Queen of Wands out of her Palace—and it's going to be you. She can't have you back in the City, Charity, let alone in the House of Wands when they would see you'd been exiled, and know she'd lied about it—she'll naturally need to kill you."

"Naturally," I said, suppressing a shudder. I finally sat down, calmer now that we were talking business. The Knight of Swords stayed away, by the cases, his head bowed. I kept him in my peripheral vision.

"And we're going to give her the opportunity to do so," said the Queen.

"Does this plan involve Charity living through said opportunity?" I asked, hoping I sounded more sanguine than I felt.

"Naturally," said the Queen, with an arched eyebrow. "You're a Sword."

The way she said it was odd, like it was so obvious an answer that it was strange for me to ask. That was more reassuring than anything else.

As she said it though, I felt something strange in the back of my mind—a pressure. My vision blurred. I blinked and it cleared. Something had upset me last night... what had...

My mother had set a seal over me to keep me from remembering the death of my father. I held onto the thought and the pressure retreated. With an effort, I picked up the thread of the conversation.

"So I'm the bait," I said.

"Indeed."

"And I'm the trap," said the Knight of Swords—he spun around at his place by the cases, fury in his face. He wasn't volunteering for the position. He was demanding the honor.

"No," said the Queen of Swords to her Knight.

"Why not?" he snapped, angry.

"Because I believe this is best," said the Queen, daring him to contradict her. The Knight rocked back, moving to pace the space between a few display cabinets—but he didn't argue, which surprised the hell out of me.

"Now, Charity," she continued. "If you were alone in the City, why would you reach out to meet her? What would she believe that you would want to do?"

"To kill her," I said with a forced shrug. I disliked trying to think like her, partially because it wasn't difficult. My mother would believe I'd want to kill her, certainly. But did I, really? I hated her. I was furious with her and I had my restored memory of trying to do so seven years ago. I knew I couldn't beat her in a duel though and that I wouldn't get the chance to try—so what? Would I stab my mother in the back? Was I capable of that? I didn't know.

Besides, it seemed odd to be considering matricide when the Knight of Swords clearly had no such complicated feelings.

"Not something you can ask her to come and negotiate in good faith," said the Queen of Swords. "If you were trying to kill her on your own, what would you tempt her with? A promise to leave the City?"

"She won't believe I'd leave her and the City alone," I said. "Anyway, I couldn't if I wanted to—I'm still on the Fool's Path and everything,"

I wasn't about to leave my mother to manipulate the House of Wands, and I sure as fuck wasn't leaving Delia in her hands. She wouldn't believe either thing for a minute.

"You didn't know you were still on the Path until we told you," pointed out the Queen. "Your time in the mundane world has clearly given you some blindspots where magic and the City are concerned." I chuckled. There were fewer of those now that I had my memories returned. Would she try to hit me with a seal? Take away those memories again or kill me from a distance? Could she do that?

I calmed myself. If she could do that, she would have murdered all the Swords from a distance long ago.

My vision blurred again—a sudden headache rising from the base of my skull. I shook my head violently, anger filling me. My new memories twisted away, feeling far off and indistinct for a moment. I called them back sharply: my mother set a seal over me to keep me from remembering why my father died. This had to be my mother trying to redraw the seal on me. Once more the pressure faded, unable to find a hook in me. Maybe it was hard to restore something like that—maybe the wards on the Palace of Swords helped.

The Queen had continued speaking while I was distracted: "I believe she could be convinced that you were unaware of your place on the Path," she said. "Especially given the secretive nature of the High Priestess. So what will she expect you to want?"

I knew what the answer was, but didn't want to say it. I knew what I would try to do, if I'd somehow survived being exiled without the House of Swords. The silence stretched, and I realized horribly, that the Queen of Swords knew the answer too— it was in her eyes, and then she said it:

"Delia."

My hands tightened on the arms of my seat. I noticed, belatedly, that I'd pulled magic in as I got angry about my mother's attempts to control me. Now, more anger and magic surged in me.

The Princess of Swords glanced between the two of us.

"Your friend?" asked the Princess.

It wouldn't have helped to deny it.

"I'd want her to let Delia go. She'll be expecting that. She'll be expecting me to do something stupid about it too," I flinched. "But I'm not putting Delia in danger."

My voice came out colder, more dangerous than I'd meant it to. The others looked at me. I should try to calm down and put the power away. I didn't.

"She's already in danger," pointed out the Queen. "If—as you said—your mother knew you were there last night, then she'll surely know this is a hold on you."

"Yes—and I have to let Delia know," I said. "I need to actually tell her right now, not reach out to my mother to talk about it. She could be..." I veered sharply away from that thought. "I need to warn her, now."

"You aren't a Wand anymore, Charity," said the Queen of Swords in a warning tone.

"Neither is Delia," I snapped. "I understood why I couldn't do it before, but she's in danger now. Delia needs to know I'm alive and that my mother tried to kill me. She needs to get out of the Palace of Wands."

"It could work," said the Princess. "Surely any message sent would be intercepted by the Queen. If Charity can convince this Delia to get out of Wands, we can give her sanctuary. She'll be followed when she escapes. Likely by the Queen—"

"No!" I shouted. Why didn't they see? "I'm not bringing her into it! I won't tell her in a way that's meant to go astray or be intercepted. She needs to actually be told I'm alive without tipping off the Queen of Wands. She needs to know before the Queen of Wands knows that she knows to give her a chance."

The headache returned. Could she stop already? My memories were mine again.

"Charity..." The Princess tried to calm me down. The Knight had stopped pacing and was watching me closely with an expression I couldn't read.

"Say I do send word that's intercepted," I ran over the Princess's words, still with my voice raised, magic roiling through me as I ignored my blurring vision. "That gives you one shot, with Delia maybe in the middle of it—on the slim chance that my mother comes herself to see me without *knowing* it's me—without knowing if I have anything else up my sleeve. She's sure to smell a trap all over this. What if you don't kill her? What if she sends the Ten instead?"

"If we can take out the Ten, all the better," snapped the Queen of Swords. "Removing her will put pressure on and probably collapse many of the seals that you saw her maintaining. It will weaken the Queen of Wands considerably, if the Ten is really supporting her so strongly."

I shook my head. Fucking seals.

"I won't do it," I said. "I'm not doing anything to put Delia in more danger. She needs to know now, or we need to force the Queen out of her palace today. Before she can think about how to beat me."

"How do you suggest we do that?" asked the Queen of Swords. She was angry too, I could see. She showed it differently. "Charity, I thought you understood that removing the Queen of Wands was a necessity for the House of Swords. It will not be risked because some mundane woman might get hurt. I will try to keep her safe—but not above a Sword. Not above my Court. Not above destroying the Queen of Wands."

"I don't give a shit about destroying her, if I lose Delia in the process." *Or the Knight of Wands, or the King. Hell, I'd save these assholes lives over killing the Queen if I was given that choice.*

"The Queen's not worth it."

They stared at me. I tried to take a calming breath. I'd

been shouting for awhile—leaning on my anger to fight that feeling of losing my new memories again.

"Charity," said the Princess of Swords. "For the House—this House, your House—there's a greater good. Have you forgotten the bodies in the throne room?"

I had. Remembering didn't change my mind.

"You will serve your House," said the Queen of Swords. When she said it, I felt the weight of the pronouncement ripple through me—through my air magic and the part of me that had been remade into a Sword. I panicked, feeling that, haunted by the fucking lies my mother was still trying to sew over my eyes with magic.

I bridled visibly—standing up and jerkily reaching for my deck.

It was a mistake. They'd been on edge, of course, since I'd gotten angry and started holding onto magic. I should have explained when I had the chance. A stupid mistake.

Magic hit me from three sides—I recognized at least one spell as the four of swords as it sent me to sleep.

TWENTY-FOUR

Not Friends, But Allies

"WAKE UP, CHARITY."

I obeyed, but it was hard. I felt groggy. I forced my eyes open because I knew there was something that needed to be done. There was something I had to focus on.

"I need to get out of here," I said, not sure who I was talking to.

"That's the plan," said the voice, and now I recognized it. The Knight of Swords. What the fuck was going on?

I sat up. We were in my room, and he was standing over me—framed by the canopy of the bed.

"Give yourself a minute," said the Knight of Swords, stepping back and walking the room. His pale hair was loose around his face. I recognized Camilla sitting on the floor by the door. She was snoring gently. Something was very, very wrong.

Delia. I had to warn Delia before my mother decided what to do.

"Sir?" I asked, fitting together the events of last night—what I hoped was last night—and the meeting with the Queen of Swords. When was it now? I looked at my window. Sunset.

The Knight stood in the center of my room, looking down at his hands. He was wearing black—which I'd never seen before. His dark cloak and his white blonde hair made him look slightly vampiric. The silence stretched and he finally let out an exasperated breath.

"My Queen—our Queen—won't give me a chance to fight the Queen of Wands."

"I—yeah," I said. "She didn't."

"She won't give you the chance to save your friend either. You'll have to rely on others. You don't like that."

I sure didn't like that one fucking bit.

"Neither of us wants to trust this to others," he said. "I know that you've no reason to trust me, and we don't like each other—" he gestured in frustration. "Just— help me get into the Palace of Wands," he said.

"Oh shit," the words slipped out before I could help it.

He blinked, confused. "Does that mean 'yes' in your mundane world?"

"No, I mean— You want to go into the Palace of Wands and kill her. The two of us?" I'd finally caught up.

"Just me. Get me in and I'll do the rest," he said it with urgency. He *meant* it. "She won't expect *that*. Get me in and you can rescue your friend yourself."

"You'll get killed," I said. "They'll burn you to a crisp

before you get anywhere near her and if you do get to her she'll destroy you with the Tower."

"What do you care?" he asked, and then didn't give me time to answer. He stepped back to the bedside and reached behind himself. He brought out a tarot deck and offered it to me.

I took the deck, gingerly, not taking my eyes from the Knight of Swords. He was close enough that I could smell the storm on him—the way I had the first time we crossed paths.

"I can do this," he said—hearing the strength of the belief in his voice made it hard not to trust him.

It would get me out of the Palace of Swords. And if we could both get into the Palace of Wands, I could get Delia...

"How?" I asked.

"I've a few tricks up my sleeve," he said. He wasn't going to tell me. "We have to go now. I'll not give you a chance to betray me."

"Me, betray you?" I asked. "When has treachery been my thing, exactly?"

He didn't answer.

I glanced down at the deck in my hand, trying to think it through, but the truth was I'd made up my mind.

I put the deck in my pocket and rolled my legs off the bed.

"Let's go," I said.

"Good," said the Knight. He gestured to the desk where there was a bundle of black cloth. "Put these on and we'll be on our way."

I got up and pulled the black aside—it was a cloak— and revealed a shirt and pants in red and orange.

Wands clothing.

TWENTY-FIVE

Safe Passage

I DRESSED IN WANDS RED AND orange and then put the black cloak over the top of that. The Knight of Swords and I left Camilla locked in my room—I felt guilty about that.

Having kept me a secret within the Palace of Swords came in handy as we escaped. I left the hood down and followed the Knight of Swords at two paces behind, eyes downcast. No one stopped the Knight as we took an elevator down to the ground floor. I realized how long it had been since I'd walked on the actual earth and got a little giddy.

I'd been semi-conscious when I took this route the first time, and I had to exercise extreme self-control not to crane my head like a tourist as we reached the open atriums and great halls of the first floor. We passed under soaring white and pink arches. Walls of marble inlaid with silver and gold surrounded me. I took it in with my peripheral vision. The whole place felt like a palace in the sky, cloud-like and permanent at the same time.

I was determinedly not staring at all this glorious celestial architecture when we passed the guards—leaving the Palace—and ran into Hector.

He didn't see me at first, focusing on the Knight as he called out, "Sir," in a formal and friendly greeting. He saw me a second later, his eyes going wide. Hector knew immediately that something was wrong—but I thought he didn't know what. Under my cloak, my hand twitched to my deck.

The Knight didn't slow his step—he kept walking out into the City night.

Hector trailed along, confused and a little hurt. "What's going on, Charity?" he asked.

I shook my head.

"Sir!" he called again, getting in front of the Knight of Swords. "What's going on?"

The Knight stopped, his gaze past Hector's shoulder.

"Move," he said. "I have business to be about tonight."

"What business?" asked Hector. "Where are you going?" It surprised me, how easily he questioned the Knight. And even as he asked the question, it clicked in Hector's eyes and he said, "No... not alone."

The Knight looked at him. I couldn't see his face, but I could see Hector's. His expression was pained, scared and worst of all, he understood the Knight—there was empathy in his eyes.

"Hector," said the Knight. "Please."

Hector wavered—and I remembered the way he'd described his card, the two of swords, and how he was with choices. I saw him wavering, swaying like his silver earrings.

"He's not alone," I said to Hector. Part of me hoped that Hector would stop us—our plan, or lack of plan, had my nerves jumping—but I wouldn't sabotage us. I tried to tilt the decision our way.

Hector flinched and didn't look at me. He finished making the decision and said, "I'm going to tell them."

I expected the Knight to react with fury, but he just nodded—understanding too.

"Then go," said the Knight.

There were guards within easy call, but Hector didn't go to them.

"Don't get yourselves killed," he said.

Hector skipped aside and started running for the elevators. The Knight sped up, but didn't start to run. As we cleared the doors of the Palace, I glanced back—I couldn't help it—the elevator doors closed over Hector.

"What was that?" I asked, confused. "Why didn't he..." I indicated the guards nearby.

"Because I asked," said the Knight. "Because he's a friend."

"So is he going to go tell the Queen?"

"Yes," said the Knight, grimly. "That's his duty. Hurry." He picked up the pace, and the two of us ran through the Swords' part of the City. I tired quickly—cardio, if I survived this, I was really going to need to start doing cardio. As I was thinking that I was going to have to eat my pride and ask the Knight to stop for a minute he slowed.

"This is the border," said the Knight. He took his sword from his hip—his focus—and held it under his cloak with one arm, hiding it. He looked back at me, face bathed in red light from a string of lanterns above us.

"Where now?" he asked.

I pulled a card from my deck—the two of wands. I wasn't sure if this was going to work—since I wasn't part of the House anymore. Still, I let my mind drift and my feet with it.

We walked in our own bubble of silence—grim and dreamlike through the City. I didn't like the idea of him behind me. Probably something I should have thought of before this.

I thought about making a run for it—just sprinting away from the Knight of Swords. But what, really, was the point of that? I would be alone in the City, with both the Houses of Wands and Swords irritated with me and no closer to warning Delia. What could I do on my own? And maybe the Knight would succeed.

He won't, I told myself. *There's no way.*

So what was I doing here?

We made it to the correct empty street, the cobbled road beneath us and the houses around full of warm lights. I held up the two of wands and the princess of wands to unlock the door, and—somewhat to my surprise—the door opened. I was about to step into the passage, but the Knight put out a hand.

"Me first," he said.

"Why?" I asked.

"Because I'm more likely to survive a trap than you are. The Wands will know we're here as soon as we cross into their Palace."

I let him go first.

TWENTY-SIX

With Skulls to Witness

INSIDE THE DARK PASSAGE, the Knight of Swords used the ace of wands to light our way—seeing him use fire magic was bizarre and unsettling. The small flame in his palm sent shadows dancing around the skulls that formed the walls. We kept up a steady pace. The passage was longer than I remembered. We strode past the sightless eyes of the skulls and didn't speak.

The skulls set me on edge, heartbeat rising and adrenaline kicking through me. Rationally, I knew that the danger of this place had come from my mother and the Ten. My body, however, just remembered that this was where I'd almost died.

Since the Knight had awakened me, I hadn't felt any push from my mother to try and set the seal back in place over my memories. I tried not to let my worries distract me.

I didn't see whatever sign the Knight was searching for, but he slowed and then put up a hand to stop me.

"We need to move quickly after this," he said. "They're going to know we're here."

"What do you mean?" I asked. "Why?"

The Knight pulled three cards in answer.

I'd gotten better at using cards, in my brief time in the City—and I'd heard enough people talk about the prowess of the Knight of Swords to know he was better than most Court Cards, which was saying something. And yet, it was different to see him casually draw the three cards needed and then use them.

He held the ace of wands, the eight of cups—a card that showed a figure contemplating a dark and lonely road—and his own card, his personal knight of swords.

He called up the power of all three cards at once, weaving a spell that demanded safe passage on a difficult journey and bent the power of the Ace of Wands itself to allow us through. He tied it together with himself, weaving his own person, confidence, and power into the spell. It didn't look like much—he just held the three cards out in front of him like any other spell. The hair at the back of my neck prickled with the abrupt buzz of power in the hallway, and my eyes watered—stinging like I was chopping onions. I tried to follow what he was doing, understand it, but it was too intricate and fast for me to pick apart.

Four points in the passage directly ahead of him began to glow—one in each wall, one in the ceiling and one in the floor to form a diamond. There were cards embedded there in the walls themselves to defend the

Palace of Wands from precisely the sort of intrusion we were trying.

The glow intensified—fire and air running up against each other, the fire trying to devour the air before the air could snuff it out.

The Knight of Swords clicked his teeth in irritation and suddenly the four cards in the walls went out. Quenched.

"Go now," he said, remaining still, his cards held in the Swords' style, while he maintained the spell. I stepped forward, shivering as I crossed the place where the dead cards were.

He followed me, crossing the boundary of the House, and then he let the spell go. He jogged forward faster now, still searching for any traps and lighting the occasional lamp as we went.

In the faint light, I asked, "How the hell did I survive when you tried to kill me?"

"The whim of the Fool," he said, entirely serious. "For which I am now grateful."

I swallowed, wishing I weren't alone with him.

"Hurry. They'll know one of the wards went down."

As we moved, approaching the end of the passage, I began to get more nervous about the lack of obstructions. Albeit, that spell of the Knight's was serious magic, but my mother shouldn't have expected him... she was expecting me. I thought—guessed—that the spell the Knight had broken had to do with keeping *Swords* out. Or maybe all other suits. Not a certain exiled Charity.

My mother would have thought of this passage—I was sure of that. There must be some trap here meant for me.

Maybe she'd left something nasty for me in the house at the other end of the passage?

I slowed, giving the Knight space and staying alert—even though I wasn't sure what I was on guard against exactly.

Without warning, the Knight whirled to face me. I jerked away, but he grabbed my arm and flung me behind him, managing to draw his sword at the same time. I scraped against the skulls and fell hard, swearing and scrambling to get up and see what the fuck was happening.

I heard the Knight's sword crash against metal, the shuffling footsteps of a fight, and then I got a glimpse at his opponent over his shoulder.

It was the Ten, her starkly pale face floating in the dark of the passage, now wreathed in flames.

She'd been behind me. My knees sagged with sudden horror at that thought.

In the narrow space, neither the Knight nor the Ten could maneuver and it was hard to see what was going on. They'd each summoned up a bulwark of their element—his air magic whipped her flames and kept them at bay. All my life, I'd been accustomed to controlling fire and being mostly comfortable with it. For the first time, I saw the menacing orange and yellow flames as mortally dangerous—felt the heat and didn't want it anywhere near me.

I retreated—I didn't want to trip the Knight of Swords if he needed to move.

They shoved and struggled back and forth in the passage—sword and wand connecting. He fought with the same conservative strikes he'd used against the Princess of Wands, but the Ten of Wands was better than the young

Princess had been. She didn't press him—just kept him thinking, moving.

Playing for time.

I reached for my deck—I wasn't thinking of any particular card, I just wanted something to help. I drew the four of swords—and felt some satisfaction at the grim irony of using that card against the Ten. I kept it down by my side, hoping that she was distracted enough by her fight with the Knight that she wouldn't see my attack coming. I'd only used it to heal myself before this, but I'd been knocked by it twice too, and I was fairly confident I could do this. I pushed power through the card and focused on putting the Ten of Wands to sleep.

She stumbled, hit squarely by my magic and shook her head. She recovered a moment later, but it was too late.

The Knight of Swords—as soon as she missed a step— ran her through.

He stepped back, drawing a card with his off hand and holding it up—to ward off any final retaliation by the Ten.

She swayed and fell against the wall with a soft groan—it was the first time I'd seen her bend, even a little bit, under all those burdens. I couldn't see any blood against the black of her coat, but I saw it drip down to form a pool of shadow beneath her.

She stared venom at me, over the Knight's shoulder.

The Ten reached for one last card, slipped and caught herself against the wall. She fumbled the card, and it fluttered to the ground. Eyes still wide she tumbled sideways and lay still. The Knight of Swords turned away. I didn't.

"Move. We need to hurry," he said.

I'd put away my four of swords and had another card in my hand. I hadn't even realized I'd drawn it. The ten of wands.

"Is she dead?" I asked.

"She will be in a minute," he said. "She was stalling—I'm not getting bogged down fighting guards in this place."

"I know— I—," I stopped. I pressed myself against the passage to let him pass me. "Go on," I said. "I'll follow you."

He saw the card in my hand and shook his head, but he passed me, saying: "We may not meet again. Don't wait for me, if you find your friend. Get out however you can."

I wish that I'd had something profound to say, something meaningful to sum up the strange relationship I'd had with the Knight of Swords to this point, but all I could think was that I would definitely never see him again. He was gone before I said anything, disappearing up out of the secret passage without looking back.

I almost followed immediately anyway. Any delay here meant Delia was in more danger. He was right, I had to hurry.

Still...

I walked carefully to where the Ten lay, wary that she might spring up. *Fine line between fast and stupid, my dear*, I heard the Queen of Swords say again in my head. The Ten didn't move and her face was turned to the ground. Unsure of what I was doing, I reached down with the ten of wands in my hand.

I hadn't been paying much attention when the King of Wands saved the Knight of Wands at my party. He'd done something to keep him from dying with the knight of wands in his deck. I didn't know if I had that power, or what to do exactly—or why I was trying. She'd been an architect of my misery since I'd known her.

Maybe it was because though I was technically a member of the House of Swords—I'd been a Wand most of my life, and I'd been walking the Path towards being the Princess of Wands. She'd failed, certainly, to be my Ten— but I'd never thought of myself as her Princess either. At this moment, that felt like a failure too.

Maybe I just didn't like the idea of leaving someone— anyone—to die.

I focused on healing—the way I had with the four of swords when I'd been hurt training with the Knight of Swords—but the magic slid sideways off the Ten. She was dying.

I didn't know what to do.

I couldn't see her breathing in the flickering light of the few lit lamps in the wall.

I picked up the card she'd drawn and dropped. It was her own ten of wands—the one from her living deck.

The card showed the Ten—with her hair tied back and her black coat, standing large in the frame of the card. Piled on her back, stacked like a sort of skeletal star behind her head were her ten wands. She was unbent by her burdens in the card.

Without much hope, I held it out towards the Ten's body and tried to let it tell me what to do—it was her card, from her deck. Surely, it wanted her healed.

My power trickled through it—seeping into the prone Ten. It was like pouring water over ground that was too hard and too dry to let much moisture in.

She shuddered and then coughed, turning her head towards me. Blood smeared her lips.

"Tell me what to do," I said.

The Ten coughed again, more blood and spittle flecking the ground and her face. She glared at me, eyes black in the dim light.

I tried to pour magic into her—and again, I felt it roll off her. This wasn't magic I could muscle my way through.

I bit down the impulse to apologize and the one to tell her she was a fucking idiot for giving her loyalty so completely to someone like my mother.

Her eyes went glassy and finally unfocused. As the tension left her and she went still, the flames in the lamps flickered and I heard a rustle like wings. I remembered that Death is a Major Arcana.

I held very still, frozen like prey, to see if anything else would happen. No step or further sound came.

Gingerly, I lay the Ten's card on her back and got up.

I took one last look at the fallen Ten and then I followed the Knight of Swords.

It was time to find Delia.

TWENTY-SEVEN

In Which My Attention is Required

THE KNIGHT OF SWORDS WAS long gone when I emerged from the passage into the former Princess of Wands' house. I ignored all her dramatic murals. I discarded my black cloak and moved quickly and cautiously. No guards were waiting for me in the house. I hoped that my red and orange clothing would keep me from standing out. A number of Wands ran across the grounds some ways distant. The Knight of Swords, no doubt, was giving them trouble.

I focused on my deck and on Delia. I'd used the two of cups to find her before. I tried to draw it.

I drew the High Priestess.

"Oh no," I said, and shoved her back in the deck. I refocused, begging the World and the High Priestess herself to give me the card I needed.

I drew the High Priestess.

I put it back and started to shuffle through the deck, searching by hand for the two of cups. I found it a third of the way through and as I did one of the cards fell out of my deck. I bent down to pick it up. It was the High Priestess.

I stood frozen with the two of cups in one hand and the High Priestess in the other, wishing and wishing that I was just a bit more stupid or blind to the way the City worked.

It was a warning or a sign or something, and I knew I ignored the Major Arcana at my own peril—and at the peril of anything I loved. Especially when I was on the Fool's Path. The High Priestess means more than mystery as a card. None of the Major Arcana are *simple.* She's intuition and reflection and a certain amount of self-control. She's ceremony and ritual. And she wanted my attention. Now.

Oh World, did I want to go after Delia. I wanted to find her and get her out of here and get me out of here and away from my mother—who could well be coming this way right now after having scorched the Knight of Swords to a crisp.

Shaking, furious and scared and over-fucking-whelmed, I put the two of cups away and focused on the High Priestess. What did she want?

She wanted me to go somewhere, because hardly had I asked the question but my feet were moving—carried along by magic and purpose. Running along my fucking Path.

I joined the running Wands with all the confidence I could project. I was drawn straight to the main palace—

the one where I'd once had rooms of my own. I wondered if Delia had moved.

Only a few corridors and turns into the palace, I found myself in a beautiful gold and copper room floored in an intricate pattern of wood parquet. The High Priestess carried me through that into the empty throne room of the Palace of Wands.

I recognized the black and orange floor, the enormous pillars shaped like wands with their braziers all full of smoldering coals. Far at the front of the room I could make out the faint outlines of the thrones, and even though I couldn't see them in the dimly lit room, I knew they were enormous chunks of pink marble sat on a dais—raised above the room.

I stepped carefully into the room, the High Priestess's card still in my hand.

When last I'd been here, I was the Princess of Wands in Waiting. For all my anger at my mother at the time, I'd belonged here—been cheered here. Now I couldn't imagine a place more dangerous. Embers—that threatened to leap into flames at any moment—flickered ominously throughout the oppressive darkness.

I walked to the middle of the chamber, halfway between the thrones and the doors, conscious of every sound: my breathing, my footfalls, and the rustle of my clothing.

Then the card stopped pulling me.

I stood alone in this chamber, exposed, listening and on edge.

I looked down at the High Priestess.

You can't see me.

The floor of this room reminded me of something—

it was the same patterning I'd seen in my mother's seal room. I spun slowly around, thinking.

If there was a secret room here, a hidden door, how would I find it—and how would I open it?

It would be locked. But maybe it would be locked with a card or two—like the passage.

What better card to use for a key than the High Priestess, who is the keeper of secrets?

I had never used a Major Arcana card for magic—to actually *change* something. This was different from being led around by my Magus or High Priestess card. Normally, it would have made me nervous about calling down the Major Arcana's attention, to use her card. However, the Priestess herself had led me here. I was pretty sure I had her attention already.

I dropped down in a crouch and put the card on the floor, willing *something* to be revealed. To open.

The strength of any given magic depends on a handful of different things—the skill of the caster, how focused or tired they are, the card and deck they're using, their inherent strength. Believe it or not, some cards are stronger depending on the time of day. I didn't expect the difference between using the Major and Minor Arcana to be quite so distinct—it was like I'd been using a small door in a stone wall and suddenly stumbled upon the main gate. I didn't have to push power through the card—it pulled my power through. And it worked.

I almost fell down the stairs that sank into the floor— slabs of black and orange sliding down with a grinding rumble. I caught my balance and found that the sinking stairs revealed a solid wooden door at their bottom. I trotted down the steps and tried the door.

Locked.

I tried using the High Priestess to open it, but to no avail.

Go.

I stepped back up a few steps and summoned all the magic I could reach. The Knight of Swords would not approve of my bluntness. However, the Knight wasn't here.

I threw a wall of air at the door, breaking it open.

The wind of its opening rippled through the seal room, disturbing a few cards.

I smiled. I couldn't help it.

I came down into the room. All the magic bound in those seals hummed. My mother's secret spells—used for the Devil knows what.

With a gleeful zeal, I threw a second gust of air into the room, letting it expand to fill the space. Tarot cards flew like scattered birds and several tables crashed over. The magic in the room dissipated—like it had when the High Priestess freed me—sending out a wave of force as I broke a dozen spells at once. I fell back on the stairs and found I was laughing.

Unbidden came the thought, in a childish voice: *My mother is going to* kill *me.*

TWENTY-EIGHT

A Mother's Welcome

I STUMBLED UP THE STEPS, still laughing. I'd made so much noise, but I didn't care. There was something undeniably cathartic about wrecking that room. I couldn't quite suppress my giggles, even after I reached the throne room and turned to watch the secret stair conceal itself once more.

The four nearest braziers roared into life around me—the light burning my eyes.

That shut me up.

I flinched and raised an arm against the sudden light, turning and trying to find whoever had discovered me.

"Charity," said the Queen of Wands.

My heart dropped straight to the floor.

I found the figure of my mother, but she already had a lazy hand up. I threw myself sideways and fire followed, the threatening heat singing one arm. I was abruptly and horrifyingly aware of how flammable my clothing and hair was. I rolled and kept moving, trying to get behind a pillar.

Fire roared out of the braziers and then flowed out towards each other, filling the space between the pillars with a low wall of flames. I turned, skidding and sliding on the stone floor, and managed to fall instead of run into the fire.

Where is the Knight of Swords? I thought as I scrambled to get to my feet.

Her next attack was already coming when I found my feet. I threw up a hand and a blast of air shot through her fire, splitting it and forcing it away from me.

She let out a surprised 'ha' and let her hand fall. I got my first view at her.

Her golden hair hung in waves to her waist and she wore a gown of gold and black with a white lace ruff. There was something odd about her though—and it took me a minute to realize that she seemed older. She looked her age. There were lines visible around her eyes and her mouth—her lips were thinner and so were her wrists. One of the seals I'd destroyed had been making her appear youthful.

Her power, however, was undiminished, if not increased. *All that power tied up in the seals... did I give it back to her?*

"A Sword now?" she said. "So that's how you survived." She smiled. "Here I was worried that one of the Major Arcana had taken a liking to you. I should have known better."

She stalked towards me and I backed up, circling away from the walls of fire she kept up between the pillars.

"Who is with you? What other Sword?"

"Just me," I lied, trying to keep her talking. "They don't care about me either. Suicide mission, you see."

She shook her head, disappointed again.

"There are two Swords in the Palace of Wands. You think that I couldn't feel that?"

I swallowed. I'm not good at assessing someone's magical strength. It's not something I'd practiced. Yet even I could feel the enormous, boggling amount of power the Queen of Wands was holding in reserve. There was no way in the World I could stand up to that for long.

"Knight or Princess?" she asked. "I'm sure the old lady hasn't come out of her tower for me."

We'd circled until my back was to the doors—the way she and I had both arrived.

"She's pretty spry still," I said. "For an old lady. Bit like you."

"Oh, Charity," she purred. "You really don't want to do this the hard way."

She sent a surge of power into the walls of fire, stoking them higher. Sudden heat in the room pressed against me. I was afraid, so afraid, of burning to death.

She saw the fear, I'm sure, because she smiled at me and beckoned the fire closer, drawing the walls in around the two of us. I pushed back on it with air and she ate up my little wind like fuel as she came closer to me, pulling the fire with her.

"I didn't realize," she said, casually over the voice of the flames, "how much power I'd bound away from myself. Thank you for this. I'm stronger than even I remembered. Who the other Sword is doesn't really matter now, does it? I could take any one of them, since the other was only you."

She stopped walking and let the fire come between us, leaving me alone in a tight circle of angry flames.

I pressed with all my strength, thinking of the Ace of Swords and holding off the heat by what brute strength I possessed. Her encircling press of fire bore down on me—relentless and blisteringly hot.

Then several things happened at once.

Abruptly, I was pushing back not with air magic—but with fire magic. That was so much easier, so much more familiar and natural. I sent her flames rushing away from me, obeying me like old and friendly hounds.

Fire poured into me and for a moment—as had happened with the King of Swords—I found myself connected to the King of Wands.

He held the bright burning brand that was the Ace of Wands in both his hands, fire licking up his arms and leaving them unburned.

I saw, in that instant, his violent delight in his newfound freedom. When I'd destroyed the Queen's seals, the spell she'd held over him had broken. I saw too determination that he would do better—starting with this—and a fierce pride for his House and the people in it that surprised me. He'd always seemed so calm.

I also sensed his irritation at the fancier clothes he'd found himself wearing since the Queen's sway over him returned.

Silently, I asked, *How?* and his attention turned to me briefly, away from the magic and the Ace.

He grinned in my mind and said, *Fire doesn't forget so*

quickly. The Ace still knows the way to you. The shape of you. That was the easy part.

Then he was gone.

The air magic given to me by the House of Swords had carved its own place—changed the shape of me to make room for itself. When I got my fire magic back it was different—I was still formed for it. Still grown in a way that was meant to hold fire. I'd rejoined the House of Wands.

My mother saw this and was furious.

"I will flay him," she promised, and she said it in a way that made me *think* of the bloody strips of flesh she meant to carve one by one from the King of Wands.

"No," I told her, still overmatched in this fight, but not nearly so much as I had been. I could hold her here. The Knight of Swords might get to us or I might get the chance to escape.

The doors to the throne room banged open behind me.

I didn't look back, determined to keep my eyes on my treacherous mother.

"Majesty," cried an urgent voice.

I recognized it at once.

It was Delia.

TWENTY-NINE

We Wands

I TURNED AROUND AS, FROM the open doors to the throne room and across the orange and black tiles, Delia came trotting in with the Knight of Wands, calling as she did so: "It's the Knight of Swords! The decoys worked! But they can't get—"

Delia stopped talking.

She'd cut her hair—she only had a short halo of curls around her face. She was thinner—more gaunt in the cheeks and eyes.

She turned from me to my mother and her jaw set in a grim line. Like she'd been born in the City, she flicked two cards into her hand and continued walking straight towards us.

"It's a trick," called the Queen, while she walked, "Delia, stand back! It's not her! It's a cruel trick from Swords! Get back!"

Her tone was exquisite, a perfect mix of fear and urgency and concern.

Delia didn't slow for a second or take her eyes off the Queen. She put herself next to me.

"You okay, kitten?"

I could've cried. "Better now," I said, and we faced her together.

Scorn poured from the Queen. "After everything I did for you," she said—to Delia or to me. I couldn't tell. It didn't matter.

The Queen shifted her attention from us, like she couldn't be bothered, and turned her eyes to the Knight of Wands. He'd approached more slowly than Delia, and came into view on my other side, staring at me.

"Sir, to me," said the Queen, commanding him.

The Knight of Wands didn't move. He stared at me.

"Charity?"

"Yeah," I said, "It's me."

"You're alive," he said, nodding to himself. He seemed wrung out. He turned to the Queen of Wands, his hands at his sides.

"Majesty..." he said to the Queen. That one word from him to her held such begging, such pleading in it. Longing. I couldn't look at him.

Her lip curled, and she said, "She is my enemy, Sir. Are you?"

"I don't want to be," he said. "Stand down, please—so that we can talk about what's happened."

"What's happened is that I am betrayed," said the Queen of Wands. She drew on the power of her card, surrounding herself in a nimbus of fire, burning with the power of the card she embodied.

The Knight of Wands squared his shoulders, putting himself in line with Delia and I. He called up his own aura—and out of the corner of my eye I saw him wearing golden armor, glinting in a sun that wasn't there and plumed with white.

"Ready?" I said to Delia, my head buzzing.

She nodded, grimmer than I'd ever seen her.

The Knight drew his focus, holding it like a sword. Delia held up one of her cards, focusing on it—and I pulled my own. The princess of swords leapt into my hand, my deck showing the old Princess who'd died with my father. I drew on my magics, air and fire entwined in me, feeding off each other and funneling through the card in my hand.

I directed a spiral of fiery blades at my mother—fire and air working together. The attack came easily at first, but by the end I was occupied with keeping the whole thing under controlled. The power of the two Aces didn't fight in me, exactly. They amplified each other. The more fire I pulled, the more air wanted to join it. I felt like I was running downhill, and beginning to go faster than I should. And I was still speeding up.

On the other end of the attack, the Queen of Wands had two cards out—but it was all she could do keep my scorching, slicing blades at bay. The Knight had almost closed the distance between them.

He'd charged forward, fire wreathing his focus and a card in his hand, while Delia—I felt Delia adding power to my fire using the ace of wands.

I struggled to keep control of my attack as the Knight

reached the Queen—unable to tell Delia that by increasing my access to the Ace of Wands she was actually letting the Ace of Swords pour more power into me too. I was rapidly approaching my limit—and had no idea what would happen if I crossed it.

I tried to stop—to cut off power from the attack—and only succeeded because I had the princess of swords in my hand. I imagined her, and for a moment I saw *her*, step out from the card and slice through all the magic flowing between me and the Queen of Wands. I stumbled with the shock of it, jarred out of my spell, and afraid for a moment that the Queen had room to counterattack. But the Knight was there, and the Queen of Wands didn't get a chance to recover.

The Queen didn't use her focus the way the Knight did. He turned his wand into a melee weapon, using it like a sword. Her focus was small, like mine had been, and fit into the palm of her hand.

As I watched, she snapped her hand down sharply and flames rippled down from her focus and stayed there, like a burning flail or whip.

When the Knight lunged, she flicked her wrist and thin loops of flame wrapped around his focus, diverting it—pushing it aside. In the meantime, she had a new card out and with an easy motion she directed it towards him.

I usually can't tell what cards people are using without seeing them—but that one I recognized because I'd felt it directed against me before: the three of swords. Its art usually shows three swords piercing a heart.

I cried out, trying to warn the Knight, though if I had recognized it, he certainly had. He had a card up to counter already. It seemed like it mostly worked—he certainly didn't keel over the way I had faced with the three of swords—but he had to step back and seemed confused.

The Queen laughed at him: "I've already had your heart," she said. Infuriating. The three of swords would, of course, be more powerful turned against someone who had loved you.

Angry, I sent a fire ball spinning at the Queen, hoping to distract her. I followed it with a half dozen lances of flames—fueled with cutting air—for good measure. It forced her back and a sneer twisted her lips. She switched cards—drawing a new one and throwing it into the air. Fire formed around it, swirling into a tall humanoid shape. A fire construct.

It turned its head and charged towards Delia. I stepped forward to intercept it—right into the fire that my mother had thrown, knowing I would try to keep the construct away from Delia. She hit me, burning my shoulder and sending me reeling back. My skin felt hot and even though I quenched the fires immediately, a fist-sized circle of seared skin stung on my shoulder.

The Knight closed with the Queen again—flail to wand—and she couldn't follow up on her attack against me.

Delia backed away from the fire construct, card ready.

I put up a hand tried to slice the card at its heart with a knife of air. It was, as the Knight of Swords would have said, a blunt attack.

The construct ducked me, staying focused on Delia—reaching for her.

Delia let out a determined yell, holding up her card—and of all the things I would not have expected, a lance of water flew out of the card and into the heart of the construct. She was using the ace of cups. Water against fire. The construct fizzled and Delia used the ace again against its outstretched arm. The thing twitched, irritated, and swung a fiery fist at Delia. I'd recovered by then—and was angry enough to pull some real power. I scorched the card at the heart of the fire construct to cinders, turning its own element against it.

The construct evaporated and Delia and I turned towards the Knight and the Queen in time for a flash of fire to blind our eyes. It had been the Queen's attack—and as we blinked away the searing light I saw that both she and the Knight had been thrown away from each other. He'd fallen and was scrambling to his feet. She'd landed in a crouch and didn't try to stand.

She laid out cards rapidly on the floor next to her— three in a row, another across the central card and then more around those.

She was building a seal on the fly, while fighting.

"Sir!" I yelled, warning the Knight.

He and I both sent desperate and half-formed bursts of flame towards the cards and the Queen countered. We got one of them, burning it to ash, and my mother slashed a final card across her own palm, drawing blood and using that to draw a messy line to connect the others.

The Knight crumpled. He held his chest and his breathing went shallow.

Delia darted towards the fallen Knight and I sent a gust of air at the seal, trying to break it. The cards fluttered but stayed put and that was all I had time for. My mother held up the card she'd used to cut herself, blood staining the edges. It was the Tower.

THIRTY

The Fall

BRIGHTER THAN THE FIRE, lightening forked from the Queen of Wands, crackling towards the Knight and Delia and then arcing up to the stone pillar behind them. It sizzled into the stone, sending chunks of rock plummeting towards them.

I blasted two larger pieces out of the air, but it was too much. Stone thudded around them, and as I tried to see which ones were a danger, I didn't see the lash of flames that wrapped around me from the brazier on the far wall.

The Queen's flames caught me by the ankle, and tried to wrap up my leg. I struggled to push the fire off, fighting against her will.

Lightning flashed again over them and more rock fell. I saw a flash of fire, but I couldn't see them. I heard the Queen grunt in annoyance.

My ankle burned, flames searing through to my skin

and scorching a ring of red there before I could force it away. I dragged myself free, but more ropes of fire sprouted from the braziers behind me, winding out like fiery tentacles to ensnare me while I screamed for Delia or the Knight.

The Queen of Wands stalked towards me, one hand raised and controlling the binding fire—while in the other she held the Tower. She'd turned the card out, so I could see it—though I'd known from that first burst of lightning what she was using against us. I remembered holding that very card in my hand when I'd been her—watching the Princess of Wands die in her duel. It showed a figure with golden hair falling to their doom.

A figure with—

I struggled to shove back the flames—thrusting aside a handful, but one wrapped around my wrist and lower arm. I screamed as blisters rose and blackened.

"Don't do it," I heard myself begging her. "Don't…"

I wasn't going to be able to dodge her next bolt of lightning. I put up my other hand and tried to slice through the card with air or blow it away or burn it, but she had me. She knew it too. This time there weren't going to be any revelations or a heart to heart before she killed me. A bittersweet sign of her increased respect.

The flames released me while she loosed a bolt of energy from the card, blinding me. Delia screamed from across the room. I put up a useless hand.

The lightning frayed at the last minute, forking into searing branches, and burning a pattern like a broken mirror across my sight. Power smashed into the tiles around me and sent stone chips flying through the air.

My mother was frozen in shock, as surprised that I lived as I was to be alive. She turned her gaze to something behind me.

I looked back too. A wiry man I didn't recognize stood in the shadow of one of the stone pillars. He took one step forward. The man wore a brick colored coat—burnt red—and his eyes were stunningly clear and blue under short black curls. The air crackled with power around him. Charged.

I've never, in my life, wanted so badly to be somewhere else. I would have crawled away from him, but I was afraid it would attract his attention.

"No," commanded the Queen of Wands, to no avail.

The wiry man didn't say anything—just stood with his hands in his pockets—such volatile magic burning in his skin that I was sure we were all going to die. I kept my eyes down, looking at his dried-blood-red boots with all the intensity I could muster and pretending very hard that I didn't exist. The buckles on the sides of his boots resembled rooks in chess. Towers.

Oh World forgive me, he is the Tower.

The personification of a fall from grace—of the rewards of hubris.

"No," said the Queen of Wands again, but there was a tinge of fear there now.

The Tower turned his head, as though hearing something we couldn't.

A moment later came the sound of running feet, and the Knight of Swords burst into the throne room, sword in hand. He saw the Queen of Wands first and started forward—then he saw the Tower and stopped. At his heels came the Seven of Wands, along with other numbered Wands and House guards. They crowded in, each going through the same motion the Knight had—focused on their quarry and then feeling the Tower and finding him with frightened eyes.

The Queen's face changed for an instant—sure that the Tower was here to reward the Knight of Swords' arrogance and not her own.

That was when the King of Wands exiled the Queen of Wands—cast her out of the House and took away her fire magic.

She fell—the same way I had when she'd done it to me—all the strength going out of her in an instant. She fell without regard for how she landed, her neck gone limp and no hand thrown out to catch herself. The fall would have hurt—but the Tower caught her. I never saw him move from the place near the shadows to beside her. He was just there.

The Tower swept her up as though she were feather light, and vanished as unobtrusively as he'd appeared, taking my mother with him and leaving the rest of us behind.

THIRTY-ONE

Reunions

DESPITE MY STINGING ARM AND ankle, I wrenched myself up amidst the horrified silence left in the wake of the Tower, searching for Delia and calling, "Dee!"

She was already up and moving towards me.

Delia didn't stop until she had me in something that was half hug and half chokehold—and she was yelling at me too.

"I'm so mad at you! I'm so mad at you, I could kill you! You idiot! You let me think you were dead! How long were you here? Where have you been? I thought you were dead, chérie! I thought you were dead!" She was crying. Delia has this trick of crying without ever making any sorts of crying noises. Tears just come out of her eyes. I always envied her that trick.

"I'm sorry," I was saying. "I'm so sorry. I didn't mean to. I didn't—"

"Damn right, you're sorry," said Delia. "Damn right, kitten. Don't you ever, ever, ever, ever do that to me again. I can't believe you're alive. Where have you been? What happened to you?"

"Your magic is amazing! How did you learn so fast? What's been going on here? Is the Knight okay?"

"I had to— I thought you were dead, I had to avenge you or do *something*. I've been practicing like mad with the Knight. It's been so scary here. She kept saying that Swords were going to kill us all —"

"She needed you all angry because— it's a long story. Oh World, and everything is all my fault—"

"It's not *all* your fault, whatever it is—"

We were both laughing and crying and hugging each other and I didn't give a damn about anything else that was going on. Including the rather large crowd witnessing our reunion. The Wands, with the Seven at their head, stood in shock.

"What's he doing here?" asked Delia finally, turning to glare at the Knight of Swords.

He'd stood in a daze, half watching us and half watching the place where the Queen of Wands had disappeared, as though hoping she would come back.

"He's trespassing," growled the Seven of Wands. "And that's the least of his crimes." The Seven, like all the Wands, appeared more haggard than I remembered. He also seemed bigger. His face softened though, as he focused on me: "Though apparently he didn't commit one of them. It's good to see you alive, Miss Waits."

"Thanks," I said. "I think we need to wait for the King."

The King.

Where was he? Was exiling someone like adding them to the Ace? He might have collapsed too.

"Where's the Ace of Wands?" I asked, provoking a mutter from the crowd. The Seven looked at me, and said, "Best not to discuss such things right now in front of...Sir!"

He was talking to the Knight of Wands, his face waxen and dazed. The Knight of Wands was standing over what remained of the seal my mother had built so quickly. He'd shuffled the cards apart with his foot. Now he stared at the Knight of Swords with hate in his eyes. He stumbled forward, looking for a fight.

"Sir..." I said too, getting in his way.

He looked at me. "He's a bloody Sword," he spat.

"So am I," I said, without thinking about it.

Oh man, did they all stare at me.

I started shaking, jittery. My arm, shoulder and ankle stung maddeningly—and I needed to find the King and everyone was staring at me.

I raised both my hands and produced a ball of fire and jet of air at the same time.

"The Queen, my mother," I said, loudly and clearly. "Exiled me from the House of Wands because I'd discovered she was enchanting the King." I'd destroyed the proof of that now, but I was sure the King would back me up. "The House of Swords saved my life, by granting me the power of their Ace. The King of Wands readmitted me to this House when I freed him, like ten minutes ago." I lowered my voice to say, "Look, Seven, I need someone to check on the King—"

"Miss Waits," said the Seven, frowning, "You're not a Court—"

"The King!" called someone from the crowd and there was a ripple through the group. "The King!"

I expected the King to be as exhausted and worn down as the rest of them, but he swept into the room with aplomb—golden circlet glittering and step vigorous.

The Knight of Swords came back to himself then, watching the King approach with an arrogantly casual expression in the midst of his enemies. The King of Wands stopped in front of Delia and I.

He smiled at the two of us, pleased and proud and finally—I thought—himself again.

"Seven," he called, "We need to send people to the gate, I believe that the Queen of Swords is here for her Knight."

The Seven looked astonished, but saluted and set to work.

"You are our prisoner, Sir," said the King of Wands to the Knight of Swords. The Knight nodded languidly, like he was only conceding a minor point in the game.

"And me?" I asked.

The King turned back to me.

"You are a longer conversation, Charity," he said. "One that will wait while someone sees to those burns."

Epilogue

THE KING LET ME STAY IN THE Palace of Wands even though I was a Sword still too. The Knight of Swords was an honored hostage, and the King of Wands and the Queen of Swords began the negotiations for his release on the same night I'd snuck him into the Palace of Wands. They didn't seem like they were in a hurry or like they were worried about reaching an accord. It was, as the Seven of Wands put it, House war as it ought to be—genteel and honorable.

It turned out that Hector had indeed gone straight to the Queen of Swords when he'd seen the Knight and I leave. After some discussion they'd come after us—the Queen, the Princess, Hector and a whole troop of Swords. The Queen of Swords was annoyed with me—but more so with her Knight—and in the end I thought she felt that the balance between being disobeyed and having the Queen of Wands toppled worked out in her favor.

After an initial discussion with the King of Wands at the gates of the Palace of Wands, the Queen and Princess of Swords continued the discussion inside the grounds of our Palace—with two very anxious entourages looking on.

I missed most of that because I'd been taken to the infirmary, where I stood with my arm in running water while a healer worked on the burns on my ankle. Delia stayed with me.

Around dawn, a few Swords came to see me—the Princess and Hector, accompanied by two of their guards and about ten Wands.

Delia watched them warily, not sure what exactly we were dealing with.

"Charity," said the Princess of Swords. At first I thought we would only see her aloof side, but then she continued: "I'm pleased you didn't manage to waste all the work I did keeping you alive."

I laughed, "Yes, Highness. I wouldn't dare."

She glanced at Delia and I made introductions all around. Delia got a little shy then, which I'd only seen very rarely.

"I'm sorry," I said to them, "About running out with the Knight."

"Are you?" asked the Princess, lifting an eyebrow.

I thought about it—"Maybe not," I said. "But I am sorry for the way I left. I wasn't going to attack anyone back in the Palace of Swords. I was under a lot of strain and behaved badly."

The Princess nodded, accepting that apology.

"What are they saying about me?" I asked.

"You're currently free to stay with either the Wands or

Swords," said the Princess. "That's technically why we're here. Would you like to return with us to the Palace of Swords? The Knight of Swords will be here awhile longer, but the rest of us are going home."

Going home.

It wasn't my home. I opened my mouth to try to explain, but the Princess said, "I didn't think so. But I wanted to be sure." She sent a knowing glance at Delia. Hector looked disappointed.

"I owe you though," I said. It felt important not to let that pass in this moment. "You saved my life, Highness— you shared your home when I didn't have one. You were more than fair to me."

The Princess of Swords inclined her head and offered me her hand. I took it and realized I would miss her. She let the corner of her mouth quirk up.

"I'm glad they restored you to the House of Wands, Charity, whatever happens. Don't be a stranger."

She turned to go, but I stopped her, saying: "You aren't worried about *her*? I don't know if she was dead—when the Tower—"

"She was probably dead—the Knight of Swords, at least, is relieved of his oath to kill her," said the Princess of Swords. "If she wasn't dead... I, for one, do not envy those who serve the Tower. Besides which, the Queen of Swords isn't done with the matter, to be sure. For the moment, I am content that there will be a truce and perhaps peace between the Houses of Swords and Wands."

I nodded to her and she left—taking half the Wands and one of the Swords with her. Hector lingered for another moment.

"The Princess meant it, but it bears repeating—don't be a stranger, Charity Waits," Hector said.

He bowed to Delia and offered me a hand. I gave him mine, and he didn't shake it—he bowed over it. I thought for a moment he'd kiss my hand, but instead he just brought his forehead down almost to touch the back of it.

"I won't forget that you saved me too," I said—I was beginning to be concerned about the number of people I owe my life to.

"When?" he asked.

"Your card— it got me out the first time my mother tried to kill me."

"Ah, yes. That wasn't really me though."

"Yes, it was."

Embarrassed, he changed the subject, saying: "I'm glad to meet the real Delia."

"The real Delia?" she asked.

I blushed. "I might have told him my name was 'Delia' the first time we met."

Delia punched me in the arm. In my good arm.

He left— trailing blue and orange guards.

Delia pursed her lips, staring at the doorway Hector left by.

"I think I like him," she said.

Delia and I moved back into our makeshift adjacent rooms. Delia had asked for a new room when she thought I was dead, and no one had had time to repair this one— so our poorly made doorway still stood.

Alphonso was almost as pleased to see me as Delia. He leapt into my lap at once, purring his head off and set both me and Delia crying again.

Delia really was furious with me and happy I was back all at once. She punched my good arm a lot. I didn't mind. I could take a hit or two while she dealt with the weirdness of losing me and getting me back again.

The next day, she and I were curled up on my bed and Delia had dragged over the comforters from her bed so that we could sit in an enormous cocoon of fluffy blankets. I had bandages wrapped around my ankle and arm, and Delia had a few for cuts—courtesy of the falling rocks in the throne room. Alphonso guarded the foot of the bed and we'd asked for our food to be brought to us. I was in the middle of telling her what I'd seen in Paris and about the Princess of Swords when someone knocked.

We called in chorus for them to come in—but instead of our food it was the King and Knight of Wands.

They both seemed mildly scandalized and amused to see our fortress of pillows and blankets. They wore their habitual costumes—the Knight in a pale yellow three piece suit and the King back in his turtleneck. It was highly gratifying to see them both looking healthy and well and themselves.

"What do you two want?" I asked, deliberately impertinent.

"To hear what happened to you," said the King. "I got some of it from the Queen of Swords last night, but I feel like I'm missing a few of the details. How, for instance, did you find the Queen of Wands' seals? I've been trying to do that for ages. When I could remember the cursed things. And where exactly were they?"

"It was the High Priestess," I said. "She brought me

right there—coerced me really—and let me in. The door is in the throne room. I'll show you later."

The King chuckled. "Maybe she does like me."

"Who? The High Priestess?"

"Yes," he said. "When I was on the Path— it was something the old Knight said, that it seemed like she liked me. I thought it was because he had a hard time with her."

"I had a hard time with her too," said the current Knight of Wands. The Knight went to drag a chair closer to the bed—one of the thick comfy armchairs. He sank into it, in easy talking distance—then glanced up, chagrined, at the still standing King. The King glanced around the room, and chose to perch on top of the desk— crossing his legs.

"That's close to the end of the story though," said the King. "Go back to the beginning."

So I did. The food arrived and more was sent for. We picnicked in my bedroom while I talked. Delia had gotten most of it in bits and pieces the night before while we were in the infirmary—so she prompted me, added details, and asked questions when she thought it necessary.

That, by the way, was the first time Delia suggested I try writing it all down.

Early on, when I was describing the scene in my secret passage, I remembered to ask about the Ten of Wands.

"We found her," said the King. "Her body is in the chapel."

Where my mother's had been.

I nodded and glanced at Delia, remembering that the Ten of Wands had once described her relationship with my mother as being similar to mine and Dee's.

Then the Wands filled me in somewhat on what had

been going on in their Palace. It sounded like my mother had spent a lot of time lying to the House of Wands, aiming them towards vengeance against the Swords partially on my behalf—framing it as another Princess stolen from them too soon.

We'd all woken late, so it was dark again by the time we'd gotten through all of it and I asked: "So what happens now, since I'm a Wand and a Sword?"

The King looked at me appraisingly. "We're not sure," he said. "You can't be the Princess of Wands if you are a Sword too."

I nodded. "Would exiling me from the House of Swords kill me?"

"We don't know," said the King. "Though the Queen of Swords and I don't believe it would—it's somewhat easier, if the connection is newer. Say, under a year. At any rate, it's not something I want to consider trying before you are fully healed."

I swallowed. A problem for another day.

"In the meantime," said the King. "I do have something for you."

He reached into a pocket and pulled out a deck of tarot cards—which I immediately recognized as my own living deck—and the golden wand pendant that was my focus.

"You had these all day!" I accused him, as he set them on the bed in front of me.

He smiled. "Yes."

I glared at him. "Thank you, Your Majesty."

"Welcome home, Miss Waits."

Thank You!

Thank you for reading **The High Priestess's Vigil**!
If you enjoyed the story,
please take a moment to review it!

Check out www.arcananovels.com to stay up to date
with **Arcana** and join the newsletter for special extras—
including an exclusive story starring the Fool!

ARCANA
Charity's Story

The Fool's Path (May 2018)
The Magus's House (June 2018)
The High Priestess's Vigil (June 2018)

More coming soon!

AUTHOR'S NOTE
II. The High Priestess

IN TAROT, THE HIGH PRIESTESS represents mystery, inner secrets, and the gate to other worlds—including the underworld. She's often seated in front of a curtain, a serene and immovable guardian. We only pass with permission.

The High Priestess guards wisdom—but she's not overly concerned with whether that will bring us joy or pain. Her concern is with making sure that the mysteries have their proper homes and places in the world.

The High Priestess in **Arcana** is meant to be a haunting presence—ghostly and dreamlike. I didn't expect to enjoy writing her sing-song voice and ethereal presence as much as I did. She grew on me as the book did.

Personally, I think of her as having a strong correlation to the tarot itself, as a whole. Tarot cards are a tool that let us externalize all those mysteries running around inside us. It's a wall to bounce our experiences off of—a different perspective. The High Priestess, like the cards, won't tell us anything we don't already know somewhere inside ourselves. Her secrets and her wisdom are not new, but ancient. Her truths are always there. It's just that, sometimes, we can't see them.

Acknowledgements

ALRIGHT! THIRD BOOK IN THE BAG and it's time for some 'thank yous'. A huge thanks to everyone who has taken the time to read these books and share them. The first book has only been out for a little while at the time I'm writing this, but the super kind words and support from all of you have been encouraging—and kept me sane in finishing up this third volume. Special shout outs to Jenny, Clarice, Laura, Cole, Leah, Brad, and Chelsea.

The fabulous cover is once again brought to you by Silver and Kaija. You guys continue to be marvelous.

The interior of this book was laid out by my fabulous aunt, Joan. Thank you!

And to the rest of my family…

Hi! Now that this book is out, I think I'll get to see you! Briefly! Then it's back to writing. <3

My dearest Damian, thank you for taking me for weirder and for weirder still. I love you.

And finally, thanks to everyone going on the adventure with Charity. Seriously. You're the reason the work is worth it.